High Deceit

C.E. Waterman

High Deceit
COPYRIGHT 2019 by C.E. Waterman

Contact Information: titleadmin@pelicanbookgroup.com

Cover Art by N. Martinez

Harbourlight Books, a division of Pelican Ventures, LLC
www.pelicanbookgroup.com PO Box 1738 *Aztec, NM * 87410

Harbourlight Books sail and mast logo is a trademark of Pelican Ventures, LLC

Publishing History
First Harbourlight Edition, 2019
Paperback Edition ISBN 978-1-5223-0245-2
Electronic Edition ISBN 978-1-5223-0244-5
Published in the United States of America

Dedication

To the people in my life who have read and re-read my awful first drafts, who helped me make them better and who encouraged me along the way. Thank you.

1

Cindy Carroll crept to the back entrance of the warehouse, grateful early morning darkness still covered her. The door squeaked a little, and she froze, holding her breath.

"Are you going to tell me why we had to show up here in the middle of the night?" The male voice increased as he and his friend drew closer.

"Yeah, the boss explained his whole plan to me over coffee and a pastry."

"Funny, Lou." The first man laughed.

Cindy released her breath and tiptoed toward the stairs. Moonlight streaming through high windows revealed broken glass and clutter waiting to scream her presence to the drug dealers outside.

On the mezzanine, she settled into deep shadows behind a rotting wooden banister. Something whispered at her shoulder. She stifled a shriek and swatted at it. A cobweb stuck to her fingers, and she wiped them on her jeans. The back door squeaked again, louder this time. A click produced a dim glow from a bulb dangling over the heads of the two men she'd slipped past in the parking lot. She backed a little and tried not to breathe as they moved into her line of sight. A large dark-haired man carried a black briefcase. His friend brushed something off his shoulder with a flick of his wrist. The hint of a cufflink sparkled.

"This is my best suit. If I'd known we were coming to this dump, I would've changed first."

"I'll register your complaint. Stop whining, will ya? You can buy another suit. A hundred suits."

The man she'd been waiting for, known to her as Boss, and a younger man in jeans entered through the open door at the front, their footsteps a hollow echo as they approached. Cindy ducked outside the ring of light

"Hey, Boss."

"Lou."

Lou shifted the briefcase to his other hand. "I haven't seen anyone yet."

"They'll be here. Don't worry."

Three more men entered through the front. The tallest gripped a briefcase identical to Lou's.

Boss held out his hand. "Good to see you, Leon. You got the money?"

Leon clasped the offered hand. "You got the product?"

Dust puffed up from an old wooden table as the two men threw their briefcases on top. It wobbled then steadied. Cindy scooted forward for a better look, almost touching the grimy two-by-four railing. A nail protruding from the decayed support barely held it in place. She winced. Announcing herself by falling into the middle of their transaction didn't seem like a good idea.

They flipped the briefcase locks and the others leaned in. She peered down, hoping this wasn't a giant mistake. Maybe the phone call she received had been a trap. Maybe they knew she'd been following them, and they led her here to dispose of her. She crouched lower and inched closer to the splintery post. The cases fell open. Sure enough, one was full of money and the other one contained little white packets.

Everyone stepped back. After nods from Boss and Leon, the men who had carried the cases switched places, snapped the other's shut, and yanked them off the table.

Boss smirked. "Pleasure doing business with you."

Cindy slid away from the edge. What was she going to do? Where was Detective Clayton? Had it been a mistake to call him? Was he part of it? They couldn't get away. There had to be something she could do.

"Freeze, police!"

Finally.

"Everybody put your hands up and face the wall." Though she heard him, he remained out of her sight, under the mezzanine. He strode forward his gun drawn, alone as he had promised. What had she done? He looked so vulnerable down there by himself, facing seven men. When was she ever going to learn? Someone moved behind him.

She sprang to her feet. "Mark, look out!"

He swung around as a shot rang out. His body jerked, and he fell. Cindy screamed. A click sounded behind her, and she spun around.

"So you're the reason he showed up here."

She stared at the muzzle of a Glock. Everything else faded. She saw it move but never heard the shot.

2

Robin Clayton smiled at the very pregnant young woman. Smiled might have been an overstatement, grimaced was a better word. Another nursery. Why did she put herself through it? Why didn't she turn them over to Maggie? *OK, forget everything else and get into the head of your client.* She glanced around the spartan living room. *Come on, you can do this.* The pep talk wasn't working this time. Her face was going to crack from all the smiling.

Maggie stepped forward and held out her hand. "Mrs. Miller, I'm Maggie Schreiber, and this is my business partner, Robin Clayton. You have a lovely home."

Robin's face unstuck, allowing her to speak. "It's wonderful to meet you. How long do you have until the baby comes?"

Courtney Miller rubbed her huge belly. "I'm due in three weeks, but the doctor says they could come any time now."

"They? You're having twins?"

Courtney smiled that special mom-smile and nodded. "A boy and a girl."

"Congratulations!" Robin lowered her head and scribbled on her clipboard, hiding the tears forming against her will. She blinked them away.

Maggie produced a tape measure. "Can we see the

room?"

Courtney twirled and headed to the back of the house. "Our room is here." She pointed. "And the babies are going to be in here, right across the hall."

Square and of average size, with builder-white walls and neutral tan carpet, the room had no personality yet. Robin normally loved that in a new project.

"My parents bought these for us. Aren't they pretty?" Courtney ran her fingers along the top of one of two new cribs made from shiny dark wood.

"They're beautiful." Maggie handed Robin the tape measure and took the end to the other side of the room. "It'll be a great place to start."

While Robin called out the measurements, Maggie wrote them down. This simple act, so routine, calmed her. A nursery began to take shape in her head. She saw baby animals dancing on each wall, butterflies and daisies on one side and maybe some fun dinosaurs, not scary ones, on the other. She sighed. Yes, it was working.

Courtney led them to the kitchen and, unaware she was practically levitating, introduced her husband, Ken.

Robin had thought she'd heard someone pacing the kitchen's squeaky floor. His pacing transferred to the pen he picked up from the table. He clicked while Robin started to sketch her vision.

Maggie threw out suggestions, and Robin sketched them in. "Of course, this is a rough drawing." She placed the sketches on the table between the couple. "We can give you a more detailed idea when we've had a chance to put it together. What do you think? Is this the direction you want us to go?"

"Ooooh." Courtney clapped. "I love it. Don't you love it, honey?"

"Is it expensive?" Ken started clicking again.

Maggie gave her a slow wink.

Robin couldn't help smiling. They were so in sync. "If we paint the full mural with the animals we talked about, it will run into the neighborhood of fifty-six hundred dollars."

The pen clicked faster.

"However, we have some wallpaper left from another job. If you guys wanted to cut some of the characters out, we could paint the background and paste them in. It would look as wonderful for about half the cost of a custom mural. Is that something you might want to consider?"

Courtney beamed, and the clicking stopped.

Ken's face smoothed into a grin as he rubbed his wife's back. "I could help after work, honey. What do you think?"

Courtney's eyes sparkled, and her contagious smile made it impossible not to join her.

On their way out, Maggie promised to mail a contract the next day.

As she stepped out of the door, the wind hit Robin in the face, stealing her breath. Hugging her coat tighter around her, she hurried to the van, and Maggie started it, flipping on the heat.

Resting her hand on the gearshift, Maggie paused. "Are you OK?"

Robin adjusted the briefcase at her feet to avoid meeting Maggie's eyes. "You realize I just promised them a job that will probably cost us money, don't you?"

"Yes, but that isn't what I'm talking about."

Maggie put the van in reverse and backed out of the driveway. "I know how hard nurseries are on you. I'd be happy to work with Sara on this one."

"No. I have to do it." Did her voice sound as choked to Maggie as it did to her?

"Why?"

Robin faced her. "Because I need to get over it, that's why. It's been eight months since the last miscarriage. I need to do my job without falling apart every time it involves children. It's not the Millers' fault I can't have a child."

Maggie drifted to a stop, her eyes huge and her forehead furrowed. "The doctor didn't say you couldn't have children...did she?"

"No." Robin sighed. "I didn't mean that. I guess I'm trying to see how it feels to say it out loud."

"So how'd it feel?" Maggie eased the van away from the stop sign, mercifully not looking at her.

"Awful. I kind of wanted to hate Courtney though, you know? But how could you hate someone so young and cute and ecstatic about being pregnant?"

"I know." Maggie's tone lowered. "At least they want theirs. I don't understand how the ones who don't want babies get them and you and Mark, who are desperate to have them, can't. How fair is that?"

Robin stared at her hands. She shouldn't have complained and handed Maggie another reason to think God was this monster never giving people a break. And did she come across as desperate? She must. She wriggled her fingers, moving her wedding ring so the diamond faced out, struggling for a way out of the hole she had dug.

"Those two were cute together, didn't you think?" She removed her drawings from the case and stared at the frolicking dinosaurs. "These dinos would have been so fun to paint." She shrugged. "It'll be fun to paste in the other ones, too. I couldn't make that poor husband disappoint his wife when she was so excited."

"Me neither." Maggie turned into the parking lot of Sunshine Interiors. "I know we'll barely break even, but I don't care. I guess we're both suckers."

Robin's musical ringtone interrupted their laughter. She fumbled the cell out of her purse and unlocked the display. Her smile wobbled. "Uh-oh, it's the chief. This can't be good."

3

Robin and Maggie raced into the emergency room. Police Chief Donovan and her husband's partner, Peter, waited by the information desk. "What happened? How is he? Will he be all right?" The questions flew from Robin's mouth before her brain could control them.

Chief Donovan stepped forward, grabbed her hands, and gave them a squeeze. "He was shot in the shoulder, a pretty clean wound. They're extracting the bullet. I'm sure he'll be OK."

Shot. The word reverberated against her skull. He hadn't said shot on the phone. He'd said hurt, not shot.

Peter gave her a hug. "The chief's right, Robin. Mark will be fine."

He eased her toward the blue plastic chairs lining scuffed white walls. People in various stages of crisis filled the chairs, either needing care themselves or watching for information about a loved one. An older woman sat in a corner alone, arms hugging herself. Was she waiting for news of a husband? She, like the detectives from Mark's unit, some sitting, some standing, watched her with a studied calm. Robin joined them, adding her less than calm face to the mix.

She tried to sit, but a combination of antiseptic and the heavy perfume of a woman a few chairs away assaulted her nostrils, and her stomach lurched.

Fighting to keep her breakfast down, she moved to the other side of the room, breathing shallow breaths through her mouth.

Maggie dropped into the chair next to her.

"This feels unreal." Robin shook her head. "I thought I'd accepted the risks when I married Mark, and after the first few years, I didn't think about it anymore." She shifted in her seat, but the plastic still pinched. "I felt safe here. The most he usually deals with is shoplifting and pickpockets." A gasp ricocheted from her chest. "You don't think they're keeping something from me, do you? They'd tell me if it was more serious, wouldn't they?"

"Of course, they wouldn't keep that from you. Someone will be out soon, and we'll know everything then."

Robin swallowed her panic. Maggie was right, it wouldn't do any good to imagine the worst. She picked up a magazine and pretended to read. Maggie fell silent, and Robin was grateful for the time to think. With a shoulder injury, Mark would be OK. He had to be. Laying the magazine on her lap, she leaned her head against the wall, closed her eyes, and tried to pray. Nothing would come. Her stomach quivered.

The routine of a busy emergency room streamed around her. A doctor spoke to a small group huddled in the center of the room. A couple of them followed him out. Good news or bad, it was hard to tell from the faces of those who remained. A young woman raced through the doors, eyes wild and searching. She found the older woman and threw her arms around her. Good to know she had someone. Robin rotated her shoulders, trying to relax.

Finally, a doctor came through the door and

scanned the waiting room. "Mrs. Clayton?"

"I'm Mrs. Clayton." Robin jumped up, and the magazine slipped to the floor.

The others gathered around.

"Your husband came through surgery very well. The bullet lodged in his shoulder, and we removed it without much trouble."

She released the breath she'd been holding. The doctor wasn't smiling. Why wasn't he smiling?

He patted his pockets and reached in for a hard candy. Unwrapping it, he popped it into his mouth.

She wanted to yank the words—and the candy— out of him.

"I'm more concerned about his head injury. He hit pretty hard, and he has a small skull fracture, so I'm listing him as critical until he wakes up."

Robin's tongue stuck to the roof of her mouth. She couldn't get the words out.

Chief Donovan answered for her. "Thank you, doctor. When can Robin see him?"

"He's in recovery now, and we'll be transferring him to ICU in about half an hour." The doctor gave Robin a smile.

Now, he smiled?

"One of the nurses will come for you when we have him settled."

When she nodded, he left, and she started pacing. "He's not dead...he's not dead."

"Of course he's not dead, honey. Did you think that?" Maggie said.

Robin winced. Had she been chanting aloud? She stopped and sat again. "I guess so. I think in the back of my mind I figured they wouldn't tell me over the phone if he was dead."

Maggie closed her mouth. She probably agreed.

Robin sprang from her chair. Mark's parents! How could she have forgotten them? They would want to be here. "I can't believe I haven't called Silvia and Ed. What was I thinking?" She fished in her purse for her phone.

"Don't worry. Peter called, and they're on their way. Do you want me to update them?" Maggie asked.

Robin agreed and gave Maggie her phone.

"Hi, Mrs. Clayton. No, this is Robin's friend, Maggie. She's fine. She just wanted to make sure you were kept up to date."

Of course, they would wonder why Robin didn't call them herself. She glanced at Maggie, her shoulders sagging. She never would have gotten the words out without sobbing.

"The bullet's out, and he's doing well. They're moving him to ICU soon, so when you get here you'll probably be able to go right in."

She made it sound so simple. He was out of surgery, and the worst was over. Robin took a deep breath, and for the first time since she got the news, she relaxed.

About twenty minutes later, a nurse came through the door and called Robin's name. She led Robin down the hall to a door marked *No Unauthorized Persons Allowed*. The nurse pushed open double doors to a large curtain-partitioned room with a central nurses' station. She stopped at the third one from the end.

Robin's eyes moved past the figure in the bed and boomeranged back when she realized it was Mark. She stumbled, and the nurse reached out to steady her. Seeing him lying there, so helpless, caused her heart to flutter. A tube threaded into his nose, and another one snaked from his arm to a bag of clear liquid above his head. Wires stuck out of the neck of his gown and linked him to a heart monitor. Its steady beep gave the only sign of life. His face, normally tanned, now almost matched the bandage around his head. His arms rested outside the blanket.

Robin held his hand, entwining her cold fingers with his warm ones, and raised it to her cheek. She ran her free fingers through his wavy black hair to smooth it, but the stubborn locks popped over the bandage again. When she bent to kiss him, her tears fell on his face. She grabbed a tissue from the night table, dabbed them away, and dried her eyes. "You'll be OK, honey. It's going to be OK. Open your eyes now, and talk to me."

The nurse who led her back had said she should speak to him, but she didn't know what to say. She hooked her foot on a chair leg and hauled it closer. "We got a new client today." She stroked his face. "It's a nursery for a sweet couple having twins. I know I said I wouldn't take any more of those, but I think it'll be fine. Ken, the husband, was so nervous. You would like him." She babbled on until she ran out of things to say and then sat for a while smoothing a wrinkle out of the sleeve of his gown.

Mark's parents surged through the door. Silvia burst into tears. Ed's eyes were damp and red, but he clamped his lips shut like Mark did when he was stressed. He so resembled his son, Robin couldn't help but smile. Silvia's short blonde hair spiked straight out on the sides, as if she'd been running her fingers through it. Robin wrapped her arms around Silvia and let her cry, patting her on the back. "He'll be OK. It looks worse than it is."

With everything inside, she hoped her words were true.

Silvia took some halting breaths, gave Robin a quick squeeze, and backed away. Linking her hand with her husband's, she moved to the bed.

Robin slipped out to give them some privacy. She padded down the hall to the crowded ICU waiting room. Was the whole drug task force here? Nine or ten men and women stood around talking. It seemed impossible that their small community had enough drugs flowing in to warrant a task force, but Mark had been passionate when he'd agreed to join. He was the first to volunteer, and Peter right after, as did most of the others in this room. Did the shooting have something to do with drugs?

Robin stood back for a moment, glad to see the room filled with friends. They would be as anxious as she to hear good news. Maggie, Chief Donovan, Peter, and his wife, Libby, congregated in the far corner, talking. Making her way toward them, she passed another small group, Detectives David Green and Greg Williams, and the chief's administrative assistant, Beth—all deep in conversation.

"Did you hear Cindy Carroll is dead?" Beth asked. "I heard she was found in the same warehouse as Mark."

David snorted. "I want to know three things." He held up three fingers, one at a time. "Why was he in a warehouse at that time of day? How did Cindy get shot? And why did he have that kind of money on him?" David added another finger. "Oh, and why didn't he call it in?"

Robin slowed, hoping they wouldn't notice her.

Beth tipped her head his way. "What are you

saying? Do you think Mark's working with them?"

David scowled. "Well, somebody is. Somebody's spilling information. I hear the upper ranks think it's one of us."

"You don't think it's Mark, do you?" Greg asked.

"It's suspicious is what I think. That's all I'm saying. It's mighty suspicious."

Cindy, dead? Her young face bloomed in Robin's mind, bringing a wave of sadness. It was the first she'd heard about that. And who did they think Mark was working with? She opened her mouth, but the chief reached out, pulling her into his group with her friends.

David stopped talking.

"How is he?" the chief asked.

Robin took a deep breath. "He's looked better, and he's not awake yet. The doctor tells me the surgery went well, but I wish Mark would tell me himself."

Greg shifted to join the group.

Beth and David followed.

"How about you? How are you holding up?" Greg asked.

"I'm OK." Her smile faltered. "I'll be a lot better though when he wakes up. Then is he ever going to get it for scaring me to death!"

Everyone chuckled at the old joke.

"I think it'll be awhile before they move him to a room," Robin continued. "Then the doctor will probably allow visitors."

Beth's face blushed pink, and tears welled in her eyes. "He'll come out of this, Robin, won't he?"

"Yes, of course, he will. He knows you all won't accept anything less." Strange how easy it was to say what people needed to hear. Brave words for someone who didn't feel so tough.

When Beth and David moved away, Greg lightly touched Robin's arm. "Whatever you need, day or night, please call me."

She stiffened, remembering their discussion. "Thank you." Did he mean it? He eyed her like he wanted to say more but patted her shoulder and moved away.

Mark's parents came out, and the chief and Peter went in for a few minutes, leaving her standing with Maggie and Libby. She leaned forward, not wanting anyone else to hear. "What will I do if he doesn't wake up?"

"That won't happen," Libby said.

Maggie gripped Robin's shoulders. "You always say God is good. If He is, I don't think He would do that to you after all you've been through. You have to be strong and not say such things."

Strong? Her insides felt like warm oatmeal. "You're right, I know you're right. He's going to be fine."

The chief and Peter returned to the waiting room, and Robin went back to ICU and sat with her in-laws, all of them watching Mark's chest rise and fall. Did Maggie think this was some kind of test? If God is good, Mark will live; if not, he'll die? Robin knew, as much as anyone, that one can't manipulate God into getting what one wanted, but she refused to think of Him as anything but good. *Please, God, don't let him die.*

Failing to get Robin and Mark's parents to leave long enough to eat, Libby brought in some milkshakes.

Robin sipped hers gratefully, knowing she should eat, also knowing nothing solid would stay down. She needed a break. Taking the shake with her, she roamed

ICU, stretching the kinks out of her legs.

Patients crowded the area, so to keep from disturbing them or their families, she returned to the waiting area. New people occupied the room now, and most of Mark's friends had gone home. Maggie and Libby were still waiting, sitting next to a large potted plant. She should have let them leave hours ago.

Hopeful eyes looked up from various groups as she passed, other families obviously waiting for news. She skirted some children coloring on the floor and joined Libby and Maggie. "You guys should go home. There's nothing going on here."

Maggie shook her head and opened her mouth, but Robin placed a hand lightly on her arm. "I promise I'll call you if there's anything to report."

Maggie held her gaze. "I want to hear about any change. I mean it. Don't try to be tough now. You call me."

Robin dropped her hand and cocked her head. "First you want me to be strong. Then you say don't be tough."

Maggie blushed. "Well, I mean…"

Robin grinned. "I know what you meant. Don't worry. Tough isn't on the menu tonight. I'll let you know if anything happens."

Libby craned her neck to see around the potted plant. "Have you seen Peter?"

"He was in ICU last time I saw him. Do you want me to get him for you?"

Maggie stood. "I can drive you home."

Libby smiled her thanks and turned to Robin. "Just tell him I'll see him at home, would you?"

Maggie picked up her purse. "Who has the kids? Do we need to stop and pick them up first?"

"The kids are home. The neighbor's watching them."

Her two friends gave Robin a hug and left together. Robin went back to the ICU room and sat next to Mark. Nothing had changed, even his hands rested in the same position.

The doctor came in around 8:00 PM, checked the chart, and made a few notes. "Mrs. Clayton, he's stable and doing as well as can be expected. We can call you at the slightest change if you want to go home for the night. Stop at the nurses' station and make sure they have the correct contact number for you."

She must have grimaced, because he stepped forward and placed his hand on her arm. "If you want to stay, you can, but at least go home and get something to eat. We don't want another patient on our hands, now do we?"

She wanted to argue, but when she stood, the room tilted. She grasped the back of the chair. "I'd better at least try to eat. Besides, our house isn't far from St. Andrews, so I can be back fast if he wakes up. You will call, won't you?"

He nodded.

A shower would be nice, too. She turned to Ed and Silvia. "Can you guys take me home? I came in with Maggie. We can make up the guest room for you when we get there."

They agreed and headed to the nurses' station.

According to the tag on the front of his scrubs, Kevin was the nurse on duty. He looked up as they approached. "How may I help you?"

"We're going home for a bit, and I want to make sure you have my correct contact information to call me if there's any change. I'm coming back right after dinner."

Kevin nodded, asked for the patient's name, and then verified with Robin the correct cellphone number.

Feeling somewhat relieved, Robin headed to the parking lot with her in-laws.

The motion sensor doors slid open, and a cold wind blew snow into the reception area.

Robin tightened the scarf at her neck and raised her voice over the wind. "Can you believe it was sixty degrees last week?"

"The storm was just starting when we left Cheyenne," Silvia shouted. "The weatherman said it should clear up by morning."

They stopped under the overhang, Robin searching the lot for Ed's vehicle. Several inches of white shrouded the cars in the lot, and thick flakes swirled past. The tulips next to the hospital doors bent over the landscaping lights, their bright blooms shining through the snow.

"Be right back, ladies. Wait here while I bring the car around." Ed sprinted across the slushy lot, wobbling on an icy patch.

Silvia looped her arm through Robin's and hugged her close. "It's freezing out here. Who'd have believed it in April?"

Robin faced away from the wind and frowned at a car idling near the entrance. Though the front window was clear, white blanketed the car. Steam rising from the tailpipe indicated the running engine. The poor person inside must be trying to warm up before cleaning the snow off.

"It's springtime in the Rockies." She gave Silvia a smile. "I guess this is what I get for living in Colorado."

Silvia laughed. "Wyoming isn't any better. At least you don't have the wind blowing dirt in your teeth all year long."

Ed brought the car to a stop, and the two women dashed to it.

Inside, Robin brushed off her hair and coat, tapping her boots together to clean them. Then she relaxed in the backseat, watching huge fluffy white flakes slide down the window. Spring snowflakes were so much more beautiful than the frozen little January pellets. She checked her phone. She hadn't looked at it all afternoon.

A swipe of the screen revealed three messages. Two were from clients—Maggie could return them tomorrow—and one from Dr. Tracy, asking to see her. He ran some tests for her thyroid at her last physical. The results were probably in. No time to think about it now, she'd call back when Mark was out of the hospital. She lay back, closed her eyes, and let the quiet seep into her soul.

A screeching engine shredded the gentle silence. Something slammed into the side of their car.

Robin slammed against her seatbelt, and a shattered side window rained glass pebbles on her head and shoulders. Her cheek stung as she brushed a hand over her face. The back window splintered but held.

Ed fought the steering wheel for control as the tires spun on the slick road. The rear wheels slid, dragging the car across the lane, banging into the curb on the other side.

Once the car stopped, Robin took a deep breath. "Is everyone OK?" She unbuckled her seatbelt and leaned into the front seat. "Ed, Silvia, are you all right?"

Ed's hands clenched the steering wheel, almost as if they had frozen there.

Silvia put her hand on his arm. "Honey?"

One at a time, he peeled his fingers off the wheel. "Yeah, I think so. Where did that guy come from, anyway? I didn't even see him. I'd better check and see if he's hurt." He got out of the car then poked his head back inside. "He's gone."

While her father-in-law dialed the police, Robin reached to open the passenger rear door, but it stuck fast. Her knees shaking, she scrambled out the driver's side.

The other car was nowhere in sight.

Neither was anyone else.

4

Tony Rossetti wiped sweaty hands on his jeans for the thousandth time since he'd buckled into the pickup. Why did Carlo have to come anyway? He could've handled this himself. And if he did have to drive, why couldn't they take his Ferrari? Or the brand-new Corvette Tony had gotten for his birthday? It was hardly snowing now. Anything would be better than this beat-up old truck. Good thing it was dark—none of his friends would see.

Carlo jerked to a stop.

A streetlight streamed golden light in front of the silent house. A soft snow swirled in the spotlight.

Tony followed him up the walk. Carlo splashed in a puddle, and Tony snickered under his breath.

Carlo muffled a curse, yanked open the screen door, and held it.

Tony slowed. "Shouldn't we ring the bell?"

"Nah, they're not home. The wife's keeping your dad's friend away while we put this in his house."

"But what if they came home early?"

"Then there'd be lights on. You don't see any lights, do you?"

"No."

"Then there isn't anybody home, genius."

His face burned. "I didn't think of that." He tried the front door. Locked.

Carlo motioned him aside. "That's why I make the big bucks. Here, let me do that."

Tony moved away and grabbed the screen.

"The wife was supposed to leave it unlocked. Good thing I come prepared, eh, kid?" He fished in his pocket. "Here. Hold this." He handed Tony a briefcase and faced the lock. His back blocked his actions, but soon the door sprang open.

"Stash it where we discussed, and don't turn on any lights. It's a surprise, and we don't want him to see us if he's in the neighborhood."

"Yeah, I got it." A ridiculous amount of trouble for a joke. The joke had better not be on him with a bunch of people ready to jump out and scare him to death. Carlo had a weird sense of humor sometimes.

Tony crept through the living room to the stairs. The bright streetlight guided him up the staircase. From there, he groped his way to the first door on the left. Bedroom curtains hung open enough to illuminate part of the room. He headed for a door to what he hoped was a walk-in closet, tripped over something, and fell into a wall. He growled. If he obeyed Carlo, he'd kill himself.

He found a switch and flipped it. Light filtered through the crack at the bottom of the door. He opened it and, sure enough, it was a closet. He shoved the case where Carlo ordered and hurried out of the house, locking the front door behind him.

Carlo waited in the pickup. "Everything go OK?"

"Yeah. Fine."

Carlo smiled, his big teeth shining in the moonlight—like a shark. Tony pictured the pockmarked face above those shiny teeth and shivered.

Carlo jammed the old truck in gear. "I'm taking

you home, but be at the restaurant in an hour. We're having a meeting."

Tony's heart raced. His first meeting. Did that mean he was getting a promotion? He jumped out in front of his house.

Before he slammed the door, Carlo leaned toward him. "Good job, kid. I knew you could do it."

The shark teeth reappeared. Why had he never noticed them before?

Forty-five minutes later, Tony sped his cherry red Corvette to Rossetti's, his family's Italian restaurant. His palms began to sweat inside his gloves. Better not say anything dumb. Mom would say he shouldn't speak unless spoken to.

It'd be fun to see the business part of the restaurant. His father always said what he did was important, but he meant Tony was too young to do whatever kept Jimmy's pockets full of money and his life full of girls. Now he was sixteen, and things were gonna change.

The lot was full. He was lucky to find a space under a light pole. A bit of mag chloride had sprayed onto the car's gleaming red finish, so he tried to rub it off with his coat sleeve. He only managed to smear it. Hopefully, the snow wouldn't accumulate too much. Corvettes had no clearance. Maybe he should have left it home. Shaking his head, he hustled across the parking lot. The same excitement he'd felt when he was fourteen and old enough to work in the restaurant quickened his steps. Now he was sick of dirty dishes and cleaning up other people's messes. Tonight, he'd moved up.

Marketing and distribution had to be better, right? Maybe they'd use some of his ideas for the website.

Mom's sauce was fantastic, so it should be easy to sell. It must be selling well because Jimmy always had plenty while Tony barely made lunch money busing tables. Now that Jimmy was going away to college, Tony'd get to do some of the fun stuff.

He ran to the door and yanked it open, slowing to a walk in case Mom was around. He didn't see her in the crowded restaurant as he half-jogged through the dining room, taking the stairs two at a time. Tonight, they'd see he could be valuable, too. He could carry out an assignment as well as Jimmy. Though it was just a joke, it felt like a test.

The small conference room was full already. One chair remained open at the long table.

"How'd it go, Tony?" Dad smiled. "Did you get in and out all right?"

"Yeah, Dad. No problem. I left it right where you said."

"Anybody see you?" Uncle Sal smirked. He didn't think Tony could handle anything. He was just waiting for him to mess up. Tony could almost hear him now. "I told ya he couldn't handle it, Dom. You shoulda given it to Jimmy." But not this time.

Tony hid his grin. "No, Uncle Sal, you can ask Carlo. Nobody saw me. I'm sure."

Carlo nodded, verifying all had gone well.

"I think we'd have heard by now if he'd been seen, Sal," Dad said. "Carlo here says you did a good job, son. I'm proud of you."

Tony basked in his father's praise, and Carlo smiled at him. The shark look was missing, his expression almost friendly. Almost. But now that he thought about it, where had Carlo learned to pick a lock like that?

5

Robin tossed and turned on the small hospital cot in Mark's ICU room, dreaming of some unseen presence chasing her, reaching out, fingers curling as if stretching around her neck. She ran screaming for Mark but couldn't find him. She kept searching for him...calling to him...her own voice woke her.

Her watch said four o'clock. No wonder she was still tired. Mark had made restless movements all night, but each time she checked he wasn't awake. After the fourth time, she quit checking and tried not to hope but still didn't get much sleep.

Dozing off again was impossible. Her mind wouldn't shut down. Lying on her back counting the dots in the ceiling tile wasn't doing any good either. She crawled stiffly out of the cot. Her muscles ached from the accident, and nausea gripped her stomach. She splashed water on her face and glanced in the mirror. Red puffy eyes stared back. She blinked. They felt gritty.

Zipping her coat, she stepped outside. The snow had stopped last night, leaving the morning clear and cold. Yesterday's few inches lay crisp on the ground. The fifty degrees predicted by afternoon would melt it all before the day was over.

She drove herself home. Since it was early, she tiptoed into the house. Stealth wasn't necessary it turned out, since her in-laws clattered around in the kitchen. They were both shuffling and likely sore. Breakfast smelled so good she couldn't help it, her stomach growled...loudly.

Silvia laughed as she dished up a plate of eggs. "Well, I guess the have-you-eaten question I was going to ask has been answered." She reached for the bacon.

"Oh, thanks, Silvia. Eggs and toast will be fine. My stomach is a little off this morning."

Silvia's eyes softened. "I'll fix you some more tea then. It might settle better than orange juice. How'd it go last night?"

Ed looked up, not trying to hide the hope in his eyes.

Robin wished she had something positive to tell them, because it looked as if they hadn't gotten any more sleep than she had. "He was restless, but he didn't wake up."

They nodded, disappointment clouding their faces. Silvia set her a place, and the three of them ate and watched the birds beyond the bay window. The sun pushed golden rays past the aspens, and the birds flitted to and from her feeder.

While Robin helped Silvia clean up, Ed turned back to his tablet. He must have been reading it before she came home and interrupted.

She frowned. "Are you reading the news? Did you see anything about Mark?"

"It says a murder happened at an empty warehouse and a policeman was injured. They aren't giving names."

"Does it say how it happened? With everything that went on yesterday, I didn't get a chance to ask the chief."

"Peter said they found Mark after an anonymous caller reported shots fired. I thought the local news might have information about a robbery or a chase or something to explain it, but no, nothing."

"Let me get changed, and we can take my car back to the hospital. Then you can use it until yours gets fixed. I doubt they'll ever find the guy who hit us."

"I suppose he got scared and ran," Silvia said. "It happened so fast I didn't even see him. Ed said it was a green sedan. Right, Ed?"

He nodded. "The chances of the police catching him, or of his having insurance, are slim at best. I'd better call my agent."

Robin agreed. "Maybe Peter will be able to tell us what they know about the shooting. I'm sure he'll check in at some point today." Running up the stairs proved a mistake as the muscles in her back contracted. She bent to wash her face and brush her teeth. Then she eased on some jeans and winced when she dragged her favorite sweatshirt over her head.

She grabbed her Bible and another book to read and glanced around for anything else she might need. Mark's presence was everywhere. His picture of the skyline, which she hated, hung over their bed, and his books covered his nightstand and the floor next to it. Neither the picture nor the recliner he insisted she keep in the living room went with her design, but he'd been adamant about having some of his things in the house.

The closet light was on. She didn't remember turning it on this morning, which meant it was already on. Mark wasn't too happy with her when she forgot—it was a pet peeve of his. She flipped it off on her way out.

Back at the hospital, she followed Silvia into the

cubicle. Peter sat next to the bed. His eyelids drooped, and he still wore yesterday's clothes. Mark appeared the same as when she'd left. "Have you been here all night?" she asked. "I didn't see you when I left this morning."

He rubbed his hands over his face. "I must have been in the bathroom or something."

She smiled at him. A strong wind would blow him over. "You don't have to stay. You're exhausted. I'll be sure to call you if there's the slightest change."

He glanced down at his feet then huffed and met her gaze. "Actually, Robin, I'll be leaving in a few minutes when my relief gets here."

"Your relief? What do you mean?" Her mouth went dry. "Are you guarding Mark? What from? Is he in danger?"

Peter reached to take her elbow. "I think we should talk in the waiting area."

Ed and Silvia followed them out.

Ed barely waited until they cleared the door before speaking. "Wait, Peter. Tell us what's going on. We still don't know what happened."

Peter stepped to the right of the door and stopped. "The truth is we don't know either. Someone on a cell phone reported shots fired at the warehouse. When the responding officers arrived, they found Mark lying near the entrance and Cindy Carroll dead upstairs, shot in the chest. They radioed for an ambulance, called us, and we called you. The problem is, we don't know what he was doing. Did he say anything to you about going there?"

"No. Didn't he call it in?" Robin frowned.

"No, and that's part of the problem." He leaned against the wall, his shoulders sagging and fatigue in every line of his face. "We don't know what he saw. He could still be a threat to someone, so we're taking precautions. The hospital will move him to a private room soon, and it should be easier to protect him there."

Robin glanced around, feeling uneasy. Was someone lurking in the shadows waiting until they were gone so they could finish the job on her husband? She rushed through his cubicle, glad to see him lying there safe.

She stood over Mark and eyed his sleeping face. The bruising spread under the bandage and leaked to one eyebrow. She reached out to touch it but stopped herself. Could he feel pain? She caressed the sweet dimple in his chin instead. How could anyone want to hurt him?

Cindy Carroll was dead? Mark had been worried about her. He said she wouldn't listen, and he must have been right. But what were they doing in a warehouse together? Could she have lured him there?

If Mark was in the wrong place at the wrong time, it wouldn't be personal. But to think someone might want him dead was too much. She started to shake.

Peter put a gentle hand on her arm. "We're not going to let anyone near him, Robin. Last night while you were sleeping, I was right down the hall where I could see his cubicle. We won't leave him unprotected. And we'll get the people responsible. I won't stop until we do."

The determination in his voice calmed her. He was Mark's best friend after all, and if he said he wouldn't stop until they were caught, she believed him. The shaking eased, but she felt sick again. She jumped out of her chair and ran for the bathroom. When she returned, the mood had changed to a forced cheerfulness.

"What else?" she asked Peter. "What haven't you told me?"

"I-I don't know what you mean."

"Now I know there's something else. You never stutter. What's going on?"

"I didn't know whether to tell you or not, but I guess it's better you hear it from me. Mark had quite a bit of money on him in one hundred dollar bills. Were you guys planning a trip or something?"

"No." So that's what David had been talking about. "How much money?"

"I don't know the exact amount, but some of the guys said it was over two thousand."

"Two thousand? Dollars? In his pocket?" She tried to picture him that morning. Did he have it when he left the house? The picture her brain called up was of him in his hospital bed with tubes everywhere. "That's ridiculous. He'd never carry so much money around. He didn't even like to do it on vacations. He was afraid someone would steal it. We take some money but mostly use our debit or credit card."

"Internal Affairs thought so, too." Peter appeared to choose his words. "They believe it was a payoff."

"What? They're out of their minds!" When the nurse on duty looked over and frowned, Robin lowered her voice. "Mark would never accept a bribe, especially if it had to do with drugs. You know he wouldn't."

Peter nodded the whole time. "Yes, I know. And everyone who knows Mark knows it too. But IA doesn't, and there are only eight of us in the unit. Right now, they're treating him as suspect number one until they find out more."

"Great. Whatever happened to innocent until proven guilty?"

"That seems to work best for criminals," Peter said. "But the good thing is when you're innocent it's not that easy to prove you're guilty." He turned his head.

A young woman rolled a tall cart into the ICU. She delivered trays emitting tantalizing aromas to several patients. When she moved past Mark's area, he took a deep breath. "We've been frustrated at not catching them in the act. We were beginning to look inside the department when this happened. Internal Affairs is going to look hard for evidence Mark is in it with them."

"Let them look. They won't find anything," Silvia chimed in.

"No, they won't, because there's nothing to find," he assured her. "And as soon as Mark wakes up, he'll be able to tell us what happened."

They sat in silence until an intern showed up to move Mark to a room. They needed the interruption.

Mark's parents didn't say what they were thinking, although she could imagine. Silvia's face was red, and she sat clenching and unclenching her fists.

"If they're moving him, the doctor must feel he's stable enough. That's good news," Ed spoke in soothing tones.

Robin nodded. Finally, good news in a not-so-good morning.

A uniformed officer showed up to replace Peter, and they stood in the waiting room until Mark was settled. His new room was on the fourth floor, and he was the only occupant.

Robin sat in a chair next to his bed and glanced around. The room wasn't large, but it felt spacious after the tiny cubicle they'd crowded into downstairs. A small pitcher of water rested on the nightstand, and a rolling tray table stood against the wall. So, was the private room for his protection or his imprisonment?

Ed and Silvia mumbled something about calling the insurance company and left.

How could anyone think Mark capable of something like this? What if he didn't wake up before they pinned it on him? What if he didn't wake up at all, and they closed the case, assuming he was guilty? The real traitor would go free.

Wait a minute. What was she thinking? If Mark didn't wake up, she had a lot more to worry about than his reputation. She'd have to face it all alone. Although what could be worse than having Mark know the community he loved thought he was a drug dealer? She couldn't bear it. She'd move. Live somewhere else where decent people weren't blamed for things they didn't do.

Robin straightened. How could she even think Mark wouldn't wake up? Because it had been in the back of her mind since Chief Donovan called. She sure talked a good game, but when she needed it, where was her trust? She needed to adjust her faith.

Libby popped her head in the door.

"I'm so glad you're here." Robin stood. "I need to talk, and I don't want to talk to Ed and Silvia about this."

Libby gave her a hug. "Let's take a walk."

They walked by rooms with TVs on and visitors coming and going, past the nurses' station, and to the elevator. When it closed them in alone, Robin spoke.

"Did Peter tell you?"

"About the money? Yes."

"What does he think?"

The elevator opened, and they exited on the ground floor.

Libby led the way to the cafeteria. "He thinks it was a plant."

Relief flooded Robin. "Really? He told you so?"

"Of course. Robin, what else would he think? I do, too. There's no way Mark's guilty of taking a bribe. Or anything else IA drums up. We just have to prove it, is all."

"That's all?" Robin wanted to laugh and cry at the same time.

Libby solved it by laughing. "Yeah, well, Mark will have to wake up soon and give us some help."

They bought coffee and went to the waiting room. They had barely sat when Tammi, a detective from Mark's unit, entered.

Robin would probably see them all at some point today. Maybe she could question each of them to get a better idea of what was going on.

Libby stepped up to Tammi and held out her hand. "It's good to see you again. How have you been doing?"

"I'm fine, but the important question is, how is Mark?"

Robin updated her on his condition.

Almost before she finished, Tammi scooted forward in her chair. "Robin, how are you? This waiting has to be horrible." Without waiting for an answer, she waved her hand. "I once knew this person who was married to someone who was in an accident. And they were unconscious. You know? Like Mark?

His wife had a tough time. The not knowing every day whether he would wake up drove her insane."

Libby raised an eyebrow but didn't voice her thoughts.

Robin stifled a frown. Was Tammi trying to reassure her or warn her of what she could expect? Neither idea gave much comfort.

"So I can see this must be horrible." Tammi took a breath. "Especially since nobody knows what happened." She got up and paced, still talking. "I couldn't believe it! I must have been on my way to work, although did they say when he was shot?" She plopped into a chair. The force squeaked the metal legs a few inches across the linoleum.

Startled for a moment, Robin realized she expected an answer. "Uh, no. I told them it was after 6:00 AM when he left home."

Tammi remained seated, but she bounced her legs. "Six, huh? I wonder what he was doing. He wasn't at the morning meeting, but neither was Peter. He had a dentist appointment or something. I think everyone else was there." She chewed a nail. "The call didn't come in until around eight. What could Mark have been doing all that time?"

Robin's face heated, and her jaw hardened. "Bleeding."

Tammi's leg stopped shaking, and she winced. "I'm so sorry. I didn't mean…"

"No." Robin's muscles loosened. "I'm the one who's sorry." She touched Tammi's arm. What was she thinking? "Of course you didn't. I'm too sensitive these days."

Tammi put her hand over Robin's and squeezed. "It's OK. I don't blame you." She stood again as if she couldn't endure being still. "I would be a wreck!" She launched into another story.

Robin paid little attention.

Tammi was either trying to cast suspicion on Peter by saying he wasn't at the meeting or attempting to make conversation.

Libby's lips pressed together the way they did when she was losing patience. If people suspected Mark, it wouldn't take them long to point at Peter, too.

Time to change the subject. When Tammi slowed a bit, Robin interrupted, "So, Tammi, tell me. How are you and Tisha getting along?"

"Oh, we're doing fine. Tish is a good girl, and you know, she doesn't even miss her dad." Tammi plopped down again, her jittery muscles stilling. "Which doesn't surprise me, since he wasn't around much. I think it surprised him though. He seemed hurt that she didn't cry when he said he wasn't going to live with us. She looked at him and said, 'Daddy, are you going to live at work?' He later told me she didn't understand. I said he was right." She huffed. "After all, work was the last place he'd want to be."

"He wasn't a workaholic?" Libby interjected.

"Hardly. You'd think since he worked when he felt like it—and that wasn't often—he'd have spent more time with her, wouldn't you? But he always had something better to do." She faced Robin. "When you don't spend any time with your daughter, how can you expect her to miss you?"

"Is he paying child support?" Libby rescued her again.

"I'm sure I'll get some after we go to court, but I'm not counting on it. He might send it for a while, but he's never been good at long-term commitments. I plan on supporting us myself, and whatever he gives me will be gravy." She picked at her sweater. "I know that's not what I'm supposed to do. People tell me I need to make him pay, but I think my life will be better if I don't have to fight with him anymore, you know? I may feel different about it later, but right now, I'm too tired to care." Tammi rested her head against the wall and relaxed, as if all the energy had drained out of her.

Robin felt sorry for the young woman, working so hard to raise her daughter alone. And in a man's profession, at that. "It must be really hard on you. How's Bill working out as a partner?" she asked.

Tammi sprang to her feet, as if embarrassed at showing any weakness. "He's great. You know, I wondered how it would work out having a man for a partner. It's not like I had a choice for a female partner in Pinon Creek."

"So it's working out?"

"Yeah. In fact, we have a lot in common. His wife has a lot of the same spending habits as my husband. At least my husband didn't leave our daughter to go shopping." She started to laugh then stopped. "Not that he wouldn't leave her to go to the track." She shrugged then leaned over to give Robin a hug. "I'm sure Mark's going to be fine, Robin. He's one of the best detectives we've got, and he was in great shape. That'll help."

Robin nodded.

Tammi blew out of the room.

Libby looked at her, and they laughed. It felt good. "What do you think that was all about?" Libby asked.

"I have no idea." Should she keep her mouth shut? No, Libby was her friend. She had to be warned. "Libby, you don't think they'll drag Peter through the mud, too, do you?"

Libby's face didn't change. "I wasn't thinking about it until Tammi sneered at his dentist appointment." She leaned back and braced her head against the wall. "I guess it's inevitable knowing how close they are. I wanted to smack her when she asked what Mark could have been doing." She chuckled. "Did you see her face when you said bleeding? I about lost it right there."

Robin grinned. "I know. I felt kind of bad."

"Don't you dare feel bad. She ought to feel bad. Maybe she'll pay more attention to what she says from now on."

"Nah," they said in unison.

In mid-giggle, Daisy, Bill's wife, walked in the door. "Yeah, she ought to watch what she says about other people."

6

Shame engulfed Robin when she realized what Daisy must have overheard. "Daisy," she croaked. "It's so good to see you."

Libby's face flamed scarlet. "Um, yeah. Come on in."

Daisy entered, shoulders back, posture rigid. She walked stiffly into the room, carrying flowers. The light shone off her pretty blonde hair, and the blue of her sweater and skirt deepened the blue of her eyes. Although right now, those eyes were icy.

Robin didn't know what to say. How could she extricate her foot from her mouth, without making it worse?

"I'm sorry, we didn't mean to be talking about you." Libby solved the problem for her.

"From what I heard, you guys weren't the ones talking about me. It was Bill's partner." She spit out the last word.

"Even so," Robin said. "We didn't mean for you to be hurt."

Daisy reached the chair next to Robin and perched on the edge. "I just want to clear a few things up."

Robin groaned inwardly. "You don't have to..."

"Yes, I do," Daisy interrupted. "I want you to know my daughter was never in any danger. Despite what you've heard, I would never do that. There was this great sale at Macys, and I wanted to get something for a friend's new baby. I went right after work, but I got held up. And just because I wasn't there right when little Jessie got home, she called Bill from the neighbor's house."

"Ah. And Bill was upset," Libby said.

"That's an understatement. He picked her up and took her to his mother's. You wouldn't believe the note he left. Like I was the worst mother in the world. And then I had to deal with snide remarks from my mother-in-law. It wasn't like I was that late, for heaven's sake. Jessie would have been fine for a few minutes."

Robin had no idea what to say. They had stumbled into a marital minefield, and she didn't want to say the wrong thing and blow it all up.

"It's ridiculous the way he treats me," Daisy continued. "As if I'm a criminal or something. I wasn't even getting it for myself. What did he want me to do, show up at a shower without a baby gift?" Daisy shifted. "He says I have a problem, but he doesn't understand. He always says we don't have enough money. I'm sick of hearing it. We always have money for the things he wants." She took a breath. "He even took away my credit cards." She blushed deeply. "I'm sorry, I don't know why I'm telling you this."

Robin made an 'it's nothing' gesture with her hand, but inwardly she wished the woman would stop.

Libby leaned forward. "Is there anything we can do to help?"

Why had Libby said that, unless she was as uncomfortable as Robin?

Robin cringed inside, waiting for Daisy to blow. Thankfully, she didn't.

"Thank you, but we're getting along fine,

especially with me working part time."

Finally, Robin could change the subject. She jumped in before Daisy could say anything else. "Speaking of the job, how's it working out? Didn't I hear you're a court reporter?"

Daisy shrugged. "Yeah. It's not bad. The trials are kind of interesting, you know? Last week we had a guy charged with burglary." She snickered. "He tried to say someone planted the items in his car."

Libby raised an eyebrow. "Did it work?"

Daisy relaxed into her chair. "Nope. The jury found him guilty." She shook her head, and as if just remembering the flowers in her hands, she held them out to Robin. "Enough about me," she said. "How's Mark?"

Robin took the flowers and updated her on Mark's progress, glad to be safely out of the blast zone. "These flowers are lovely," she said standing, "they'll need some water. Would you like to come to Mark's room?"

Daisy nodded. "I'm supposed to meet Bill. He should be here soon."

As they took the elevator back to Mark's floor, Libby checked her watch. "Peter's picking me up in a few minutes to take me to see Virginia Carroll. She goes to our church, and he feels if I'm there it may be less stressful for her."

"Is that Cindy's mother?"

"Yes, poor woman. She lost a son to a drug related event last year, and now her daughter. I don't know if I could take it."

"I heard about that at the time," Daisy said. "It hurts to think of losing a child, and in such a horrible way. I heard he jumped off the roof or something."

The elevator stopped on Mark's floor. A

uniformed officer sat in a chair outside Mark's room. He looked familiar from her trips to the station, but Robin couldn't quite remember his name. He introduced himself as Jack Olsen. Then she remembered. He worked the front desk sometimes.

Silvia sat next to Mark's bed, stroking his shoulder. She must have been talking to him, trying to wake him.

Ed sat in the recliner nearby, reading some kind of trade magazine.

Mark looked the same as before, his face still pale against the pillow. Robin picked up his hand, the one without the IV, and brought it to her lips. It was warm, despite resting outside the blankets. She fought the urge to tuck the covers more securely around him for fear of dislodging any tubes, and lowered his hand to its former position.

"Please wake up, sweetheart," she said, tears forming in her eyes again. "I need you." She focused on his face as if the two of them were alone. But a rustle behind her reminded her of everyone else in the room. "We all need you."

7

After a three-hour nap, Peter woke with a headache. His body wanted more sleep, but he needed to see the crime scene. If he'd known how things would be with Internal Affairs, he would've gone there yesterday. Now, it would be harder to tell what happened, but maybe something about the scene would help him piece things together.

He parked far enough away to walk through the lot and check for anything the crew might have missed. Crisp air chilled his nose, but the strong sun melted last night's snow. The ground was swept clean, not even a piece of trash remained. He should have expected that. The crime scene unit didn't miss much.

Police tape crisscrossed the entrance in place of a door. He removed one side at the top and stepped over the bottom, tacking the top piece back when he went through. Judging by the vacant building's rickety stairs and the dirt and grime, it had long been abandoned. David said he'd contacted the owner and discovered he'd been trying to sell it but had given up hope. He mustn't have thought keeping it up was in his best interest.

Peter moved around the building, looking for obvious signs of activity. Some scuffmarks marred the dirt on the cement floor, but there was no way to tell how much of it occurred during the investigation and how much was there before. Any number of people could've been in the warehouse with Mark. He'd ask to see the preprocessed crime scene pictures, but he still wouldn't know how many were from the medical team.

A fair amount of blood stained the floor near the entrance, likely where Mark lay. He gazed up at the loft where he'd heard Cindy's body had been found.

Would IA try to make it look as if Mark killed her and then someone shot him as he was leaving? He could have hit her from this distance. But the gun they'd found in Mark's hand hadn't been his issue. In fact, it had been reported stolen recently.

Peter climbed the rickety stairs and scanned the upper level for evidence of where they'd found Cindy. The outline of her body was near the banister, and blood splatter covered some of the rotted wood. He squatted and peered through the decayed boards, careful not to touch anything. She could have been watching something below. Had Mark known she was here? Peter rose and stood back a few feet, examining the splatter. It splayed toward the rail, so Mark couldn't have shot her from downstairs. Unless they thought he killed her first, went to leave, and was shot at the door.

He ground his teeth. Not knowing what IA was thinking was so...so frustrating. Would they tell him what tests they'd ordered and their results? Probably not. If they thought Mark was guilty, they wouldn't trust his partner. He took pictures with his phone where they found Cindy's body and then hovered it over the banister and snapped a few more. What could she have been watching? A table sat almost beneath the mezzanine, and from this vantage point, it was clear that the dust on it had been disturbed.

Maybe he could get information some other way. If they used the state lab, he might talk Bob Randall into giving him details. Bob was a good guy. He wouldn't like IA railroading Mark.

Nothing else at the warehouse jumped out at him, so he took some general pictures and walked back to his car. His next task required a delicate touch. He wanted to talk to Cindy's mom, and she'd already been questioned. She went to his church, so a social visit wouldn't be out of order, and with Libby along, as they'd planned, it would be unofficial. Besides, no one was better at dealing with grieving people than his wife.

He picked Libby up at the hospital and drove her to Virginia Carroll's home. One look at the silent house almost made him reconsider. The blinds were drawn and the only sound was melting snow dripping from the trees. Peter found himself wanting to tiptoe up the walk.

Libby grabbed his arm slowing him to a stop. "Do you think she's awake? Maybe we should come back later."

"I don't think that would help. We're going to disturb her no matter when we come." He led the way to the front door before he changed his mind.

Cindy's mom answered his knock, unlocked the screen, and pushed it open. Her face, without makeup, showed every line, and her hair was squashed to one side. She forced a polite smile. "Peter, Libby. Come on in."

Peter's stomach churned over questions he had to ask. But which was better, let her alone to grieve in peace or bother her and possibly find her daughter's killer? Cindy deserved justice. That didn't make facing a grieving mother any easier.

"We're so sorry, Virginia." Libby grasped her hands. "What can we do? Is there something you need?"

Virginia shook her head. Her lips trembled, and her already-red eyes filled with tears. Libby took her in her arms, murmuring in her ear. Peter couldn't hear her, but Virginia's shoulders relaxed and her labored breathing slowed.

All they needed was for her to have another attack. She had heart problems, and losing a daughter after having lost a son a year ago could send her over the edge.

Virginia led them into the small living room. The drawn drapes made it cold and dreary. It had a bygone aura to it, red barn fabric on the couch and chair, and side tables similar to the ones in the house where he'd grown up.

The two women sat together on the Early American style couch, and Peter moved to a chair across from them. He prayed for Virginia and for guidance then scooted to the edge and touched her hand.

"I'm sorry to have to do this, but I need to ask you some questions. Are you up to answering them now? I hate to wait because the longer we put it off, the more time your daughter's killer has to get away."

Virginia gave a shaky nod.

He patted her hand and brought out his notebook. "Another policeman may have asked you this already, and if so I apologize, but do you know why Cindy was in the warehouse? Had she told you she would be there?"

Virginia twisted a handkerchief in her lap. "Not a warehouse. She called around eleven o'clock and said she was at a charity event and not to worry if she was home late."

"Did she say where it was or who it was for?"

"No, she left a message since I was asleep. She never went to charity events, at least not as far as I know—we don't have that kind of money. I assumed it had something to do with the DARE Program."

Peter rested the notebook in his lap and gave her his full attention. "What else was going on? Had Cindy been acting strange?"

Her eyes glimmered. "You mean more than normal? Ever since Joey died, she hasn't been the same. She was driven to catch the people who hurt him. She wanted them all to pay." Virginia loosened her grip on the handkerchief and stared at her hands, moving her reddened fingers as if they hurt.

Peter remained silent, not wanting to stem the flow of information.

Virginia lifted the corners of her mouth. "I was so proud of her. She was determined to ensure every kid in town knew how dangerous drugs could be. I thought she'd settle down after they arrested the guy who gave it to Joey, but the trial fueled her fire. She wanted drugs out of Pinon Creek altogether." Her smile widened, and this time it reached her eyes. She chuckled. "Once that was accomplished she might have gone global."

Peter grinned back, remembering the determined college student.

Virginia's smile disappeared. "She was like that about everything. Once she made up her mind, nothing could change it. Believe me, I tried."

"Could she have met someone on the college campus?"

Virginia seemed to think for a long moment. "Not that she mentioned, but you could ask Nora Lane. She was Cindy's best friend."

Peter wrote the name. He'd just have to do that.

8

Robin breathed in the spicy scent of the casserole Libby unwrapped for their dinner. If she closed her eyes, she could imagine herself in Libby's warm kitchen instead of a sterile hospital room. "Maggie will be upset she missed this. You know how much she loves your cooking."

Libby plopped a spoonful onto a paper plate and handed it over. "No worries. I left one for her, too—and one for the Carrolls. I was on a roll last night."

Ed and Silvia took a plate, but Daisy and Bill declined.

"We'd better run." Daisy rose from her chair next to Mark's nightstand. "The kids will be starving. I'm sorry to be missing out on this though. It smells heavenly."

Anxious to ask Bill some questions, Robin stood to see them out.

Bill and Daisy shook hands with Mark's parents.

"Daisy," Silvia said. "I forgot to tell you how pretty you look. Love your outfit, is it new?"

Daisy glanced sideways at Bill. "Uh no, not really. I mean, I've had it a while." Daisy hurried to the door, probably anxious to avoid a scene with her husband.

Robin's cheeks flamed again. Although with what she'd overheard, there would likely be a scene at home anyway. Robin waved good-bye and returned to her seat. As she wiggled into the vinyl, she almost sprang back up. She'd meant to question Bill about what he'd heard around the department. Oh, well, it'd have to wait.

They were still eating when Peter and Greg showed up in their team t-shirts on their way to the season's first softball game of their city league. The red and white t-shirts were spotless, probably for the last time.

"You guys look spiffy," Robin said. "What's the weather like? Are you still going to have the game?"

"Typical Colorado spring weather. Thirty degrees and snowing yesterday, and fifty and sunny today."

Libby dished some of the casserole onto a couple of plates for her husband and Greg. "I called the rec center. The guy told me we're on for tonight. Since the snow melted, the fields will be a mess, though. I'm not excited about this one." She grinned. "Don't you wish you could join?"

Robin laughed. "Not really. I think I'll pass this time."

Libby rested her hand on her husband's arm. "Peter wanted to check on Mark before the game, and I'm sure he'll want to come by afterward since we're so close."

Promising Peter he could check in on Mark was probably the only way Libby got him to go.

"So, Robin, are you going to be with us in spirit?" Greg asked. "We're gonna miss you and Mark tonight."

"The way I've been hitting in practice, you'll be better off without me." She chuckled. "Mark keeps taking me to the batting cages, but I can't figure out what I'm doing wrong. I keep swinging, but all I hit is air."

They all laughed.

David, Greg's partner, walked into the room. "I don't know what Mark thinks he's getting away with having a private room and all," he said. "Is that on the city's health plan?"

No one answered.

Peter changed the subject. "What did you guys find out this morning? Were there witnesses?"

"Nobody was around that early." David shrugged. "We found the guy who made the call, and took what information he had, but he didn't know much. I put it in my report, so you can see it back at the station." He moved around the bed to stand by Greg. "The witness lives in a loft overlooking the warehouse. He said he saw some cars, but not close enough to identify. Almost everyone we talked to was asleep at the time of the shooting." He elbowed Greg. "You know, if Mark was going to make himself a target, I wish he'd made it later in the day." He snickered, but no one joined him.

Robin's cell phone rang, saving them from awkwardness. She scooped it out of her purse.

"Mrs. Clayton?"

"Yes."

"Mrs. Mark Clayton?"

"I'm Robin Clayton, yes. What can I do for you?"

"Someone could have gotten hurt last night." The voice was silk.

Last night? Didn't they mean yesterday morning?

"Who could've gotten hurt?"

She gripped the cell tighter, pinching her fingers against the plastic case. "You mean Mark? What are you talking about?" The accident! Her accident. Her knees wobbled, and her heart pounded so loud the man on the other end of the line must hear it.

He didn't respond.

"What are you talking about?" she asked again.

"I think you know, Mrs. Clayton. Accidents happen."

"Did you do that? Why? What do you want?" Her voice reached a squeaky pitch. "There were older people in the car!"

"Protect them," he purred. "Protect yourself."

The line went dead. She couldn't catch her breath. Who would do such a thing? And why? What could they hope to gain? Her hand shook as she slid the phone back in her purse.

"Robin, you're white as a sheet!" Libby sprang to her side. "What's wrong? Was that about the accident last night?"

"I'm not sure it was an accident. I think the call was meant to frighten me, but I don't know what they could want." She relayed what the man said.

Libby placed her hands on her hips. "It's not enough they shot your husband, now they try to run you over in the car? I can't believe this."

"Did you recognize the voice?" Peter asked, his tone professional and calm.

"No, I don't think I've heard it before."

"What about the number?"

She pulled her phone out and clicked through the screens. "There's a number, but I don't recognize it. The coward. I thought some scared kid hadn't paid up his insurance last night. To think someone hit us on purpose!"

Peter took her phone and dialed. After a few seconds, he hung up. "It's probably a throwaway, but we'll check on it. Do you know what he could have meant? Did Mark say anything about receiving any threats before he left yesterday morning?"

Had he? "No, all he said was he had to go in early, and he'd see me later. Then he left. He didn't seem upset or worried."

"Did you see the car last night?"

"I didn't, but Ed said it was a green sedan."

Peter looked at Mark's father, who gave a confirming nod. "I don't remember much except it was older. It was dark outside, so I saw the color by streetlight. I didn't catch a plate."

"I don't think the guy meant to kill you, since he had every opportunity. Maybe he wanted to scare you." Peter tapped his pen against the notebook. "The question is why. Tell me exactly what he said."

She repeated it.

Peter jotted her words down then paused. "Do you remember seeing the car in the hospital parking lot?"

"There was a car warming up. Snow covered everything but the front window, so I don't know the color. If it was him, he could have hit us in the parking lot before we got into the car."

Peter pursed his lips. "I think you're right. He must have wanted to leave a warning of some kind. We need to figure this out and fast."

Libby patted her husband's arm. "Why don't I go with Greg, and you can join me when things are settled?"

He flashed her a smile. "Thanks, honey."

Libby and Greg left.

Peter eyed Robin. "I'm going to order a bodyguard for you and have a tap put on your phone."

"No. I don't need a bodyguard. Like you said, if

they'd wanted to kill us, they could have. I doubt there'll be any more trouble. I want you to concentrate on catching Cindy's murderer. Then I won't need a bodyguard."

Peter tried to convince Robin she needed protection. She agreed to the phone tap, but not to having a bodyguard, so after talking to someone at the station Peter and David left.

David poked his head back in the door. "Oh, by the way, the chief said to tell you he'd be by later tonight."

When she nodded, he hurried to catch up with Peter. She slumped against the back of her chair, her chest heavy. No way would she let Peter take an officer away from the investigation to protect her. They wouldn't try anything with all the people here, but thinking someone might be watching made her shiver.

She tried to persuade Ed and Silvia to leave for the night.

Beth came into the room. Blonde wisps fell from her upswept hair, and she shimmered in a black sequined evening gown.

"Wow, don't you look gorgeous," Robin gushed. "Where are you going tonight?"

"We're headed for dinner and the opera, but I wanted to check on Mark first. And on you." She peered into Robin's face. "You look upset. Has something happened?" She spun to Ed. "Is Mark all right?"

Robin dropped into a chair and explained the phone call. The more times she said it, the sillier it sounded—like some old movie or something, way overdramatic.

Beth perched on the arm of a chair, careful not to

crease her beautiful dress. "That sounds serious. Did you tell someone?"

"I couldn't avoid it since everyone was in the room. Peter wants to get me a bodyguard."

Beth's concerned gaze caught hers and held. "What could they want from you? What did Mark tell you?"

"He didn't tell me anything. I have no idea why he was there. He said he had an appointment, and he left."

"Are you sure? Maybe he said something that doesn't seem important?"

"If he did, it was so unimportant I can't remember it."

Beth tucked a stray piece of hair behind her ear. "Well, I wouldn't worry then. Once they realize you don't know anything, they'll leave you alone." She glanced at Mark's bed. "I'm sorry this had to happen to Mark. He's one of my favorite guys on the squad. I hope he's OK."

"Thanks." Robin's voice caught in her throat. "Knowing so many people care feels good. I'm sure he'll wake soon." Did she believe it? If so, why the knot in her stomach?

Beth stood. "My date's in the car, so I'd better go if you don't need anything." She paused until Robin shook her head. "See you later. Let me know what I can do to help." And she was gone.

Knowing life went on for other people felt strange. They had dinner dates and softball games, their lives unchanged. But what were they supposed to do? Sit here as she did until Mark woke up?

At least they cared enough to come. As far as Robin knew, Beth and Mark hadn't been close friends, although they'd joked a lot. Something like this brought out the best in people. Everyone was being so kind.

But she'd heard them whispering. Not only was someone in the department dealing drugs, they were trying to blame it on Mark.

When Ed and Silvia decided to leave, she walked out with them to escape her oppressive thoughts. The crisp air tingled against her skin, wakening her. They paused by her car, and she couldn't help glancing around. Complete darkness spread beyond the circle created by the light pole. No cars warming up tonight. A chill slithered down her spine. Were they watching right now?

"Come home with us. We can drive you back later." Silvia drew her into a hug. "We can't leave you alone knowing someone out there might want to hurt you."

Robin gave her a quick squeeze. "What about you? We were all together when it happened."

"They don't want us, Robin," Ed responded before Silvia could. "They've targeted you and Mark. We were along for the ride, so to speak."

The word *targeted* scuttled through her mind. She rubbed the goosebumps from her arms. "I'm far more protected than you. There's a guard outside Mark's door, remember?"

Silvia nodded. "But go right back inside." She grabbed Robin's hands and held her gaze. "And don't go anywhere outside the hospital alone. Promise me."

Robin promised, and they waited until she was through the doors before they left. *Targeted.* The word came out of hiding. Was Mark a target now? Was she? She scanned the hall as she entered the elevator. A man in blue coveralls pushed a broom down the otherwise empty hallway. Was he a janitor or something else? Her heart quickened with an urgency to return to Mark. What if he wasn't safe? Wait. The guard was there. Mark was safe. She had to wrestle her imagination under control.

Her cell rang as she approached Mark's room. She glanced at the display and exhaled.

Maggie.

"How's Mark? Is he awake?"

"Not so far." Her voice betrayed her discouragement.

"He'll wake up, honey."

"I know."

"In the meantime, maybe I can cheer you up. You won't believe the interview I had today."

"That's right. You had the bank job, didn't you?" Robin laughed. Maggie was right, she did cheer up. "Whoa. That didn't come out right."

Maggie giggled. "Well, I didn't rob it, but the security guard probably thought I was casing the joint. I have to turn in some sketches, and we should hear if we got the job next week."

"Great! It should be a good test of our talents. I have some other news." Robin told her about the phone call. A pause reverberated on the other end of the line, and Robin pictured Maggie's frown.

"They hit you with their car? Why? What would they hope to gain? You guys stopped, right? So if he'd wanted to hurt you, he could've then without witnesses."

Robin stopped walking. "You're right. I was thinking he could've done something in the parking lot, but no one was nearby on the road. In fact, if he hadn't made his creepy call, I wouldn't have connected it. I thought it was the slick roads and some guy who didn't have insurance."

As Maggie's breath became uneven, Robin imagined her pacing. She started walking again, too.

"Robin, this is too weird. I mean how can you do what he wants when he didn't tell you what it was?"

Leave it to Maggie to get to the heart of it. "Thank you. That's what I thought." Finally, someone understood what had been bothering her. "He said he thought I knew what he wanted. How can I do, or not do, what he wants, when I don't have the first clue?"

"This worries me. You need to let Peter give you a bodyguard."

"Everyone else thinks so, too. But I don't want the department taking anyone off the case." Robin nodded to the police officer outside Mark's door before going inside. "There's a guard here, and this is where I spend my time anyway. I don't need anybody else."

"That's fine as long as you don't leave the hospital, but I know you'll not be there twenty-four-seven. When you leave, you need a guard."

"I'll think about it." Robin settled next to the bed. "A few people thought I should know why Mark went into the warehouse, but I don't. And I certainly don't know what made him not call it in."

Maggie was silent as she digested this.

"Unless he thought someone would intercept the call, and they would get away again." Robin cleared her throat and lowered her voice. "Maggie, what if it's one of his friends?"

"And they want to know if you know who they are? I wondered the same thing, but I didn't want to say it." Maggie huffed into the line. It sounded as if she was jogging. "Is anyone acting weird?"

Robin laughed. "Besides you?" She crossed her legs. "You know, it seems like David wants people to believe Mark is guilty."

"You mean what he said while you were coming back from seeing Mark in ICU yesterday?"

"You heard him?"

"I couldn't help it. We were right next to them. I think it's why the chief spoke up so fast. He wanted David to know you were there and that he should shut up." She fiddled with the hem of her shirt. "He's made a couple of other cracks too—one about the timing of the shooting being too early for witnesses and one about him having a private room. Of course, some of it is David's personality. He's always been socially clumsy."

"Nice way to put it. I think he's plain nasty. I never have liked him." Maggie giggled. "It's too bad, too, because his partner is delish."

"I thought you were a little dressed up to deliver lunch."

"That was for the bank interview." Maggie's voice was too innocent. "I had to look nice."

"Uh-huh."

"But we have gotten off the subject. What are we going to do about keeping you safe? I don't like thinking someone could be out to hurt you."

Maggie could be a dog with a bone sometimes. "It's obvious they didn't want to kill us or they would have. I'm plenty safe here. If it makes you feel better, I promised Ed and Silvia I'd be extra careful."

"Call me before you leave, and I'll come and get you. Or have one of the guys take you home. I don't want you alone."

Arguing was no use. Not with Maggie. So she promised before ending the call. It seemed worthless though, since she wasn't alone the last time.

Robin watched TV until she couldn't keep her eyes open or stop yawning. A quick visit to the nurse's station for coffee would help. As she passed the elevator, the doors opened.

Chief Donovan stepped out.

"Hi, Chief. It's good to see you." She gave him a hug and walked with him to Mark's room.

He folded his arm around her shoulders. "You look beat. Has Mark's condition changed?"

"No, nothing yet." A tear escaped. She reached up to wipe it away, only to find more taking its place. To her horror, the dam burst and tears flooded her face.

He paused, and she covered her face with her hands. He patted her on the back at first then drew her into a hug. She couldn't quit. She ducked her head and sobbed into the front of his jacket. He was so tall she came to about mid chest. At length, the tears slowed to the hiccup stage, and she backed away. He handed her a handkerchief and guided her along the hall, not saying anything, letting her get herself under control. At Mark's door, he stopped to speak to the guard.

Robin went into Mark's room to compose herself. How brainless was that? Why couldn't she have had her little breakdown when she was alone? But then she'd hardly been alone all day. Maybe he wouldn't stay long. She couldn't take being nice another second.

A few minutes later, the chief came in and bent over Mark. "Mark? You have to wake up, buddy. You're scaring us." He touched Mark's shoulder, bumping against the bed. His keys clattered to the floor in the quiet room.

Robin jumped, startled.

He bent to pick them up. When he stood, his face was red, whether from bending over or from embarrassment, she couldn't tell.

"Sorry. I didn't mean to give you a heart attack." He tucked them into his pants pocket. "I took my other coat to the cleaners. These pockets aren't deep enough and things fall out."

Robin laughed and followed him to the door of Mark's room to say good-bye. As he strode away, the word *targeted* slithered into her mind. The chief couldn't be the one, could he? He appeared to care about his people. And Mark liked and respected him. But how could she be sure? Could she trust him? Maybe it was all a show. Or maybe he did like Mark, but he liked money more.

The cot had clean sheets folded on it when she returned. She made the bed and tried to sleep, but her mind wouldn't stop. What about David? Was he trying to cast suspicion on Mark, or was he plain dense?

Tammi threw suspicion on Peter for not being at the morning meeting. Mark told her Tammi had a fear of hospitals. Was that all? Or was she trying to divert suspicion?

~*~

Mark drifted in a sea of dark clouds. That voice. When he'd heard it today, he'd panicked. He tried to move, but he couldn't. Why couldn't he see? He tried to force his eyes open. The haze began to lighten. He had to warn Robin. She didn't know about the snake slithering among them, feeding off their misery.

She was in danger, he could feel it. And he was helpless. He struggled to climb out. The mists closed in again. Wait, what was it he wanted to tell her? He began to relax. All was warm and comfortable as he slid back under.

9

Tony's shift was almost over. It was nearly eleven, and he was just finishing up. His arms ached from the heavy bus tubs. The last table had been the worst. Twin two-year-olds. The clean-up from that had taken nearly half an hour. He had a few last areas to wipe down, and he could go home for the night. He wrung out his rag and headed for the last booth.

Carlo appeared out of nowhere. "Hey kid, you're wanted upstairs."

Tony jumped, nearly dropping the rag. "Me?"

"Yeah. Ditch the rag and go up to the conference room. We're having a meeting."

"OK, be right there." His pulse picked up. He was finally being invited to a meeting about the business. He dumped the rag with the others to be laundered, slipped out of his apron and hoped he didn't smell like spaghetti sauce. Although, the whole place smelled like sauce, so he guessed it wouldn't matter.

He took the broad stairs two at a time and went down the hall to the conference room. Everyone was there. He took a seat next to Jimmy, about halfway down the long table. Dad slipped in and sat at the end, avoiding eye contact. It was obvious he didn't want to be here. Probably too busy running the place to waste time in a meeting. Tony stared at him, hoping he'd glance up.

Carlo strutted in. There was no other word for it--strutted. As if he had rap music playing in his head. He took the empty chair at the opposite end as Tony's dad. Tony studied him. He wasn't tall, five-six or so, about Tony's height. But he wore arrogance like a suit.

Dad planted his elbows on the table, bracing himself. "You can't do this, Carlo."

Carlo smirked. "Do what, Dominic?"

Jimmy cleared his throat.

Dad's eyes traveled down the table and found his. "Tony, what are you doing here, son? Doesn't your mother need you downstairs?"

Uncle Sal snickered.

Tony felt his face grow warm. Everyone's eyes were on him. He opened his mouth to defend his right to be here.

"I asked him to come." Carlo rescued him. "If he's going to be taking more responsibility, he should understand the business better. Right, boy?"

"Right, sir." Ugh. Why had he called him that?

Dad sat back in his chair, seemingly tongue-tied.

"So let's call this meeting to order," Carlo said. "We're here to discuss oregano."

Dad's face went slack. "Oregano?"

"Yeah. The problem we're having getting our shipments of oregano. Our vendor is having a hard time getting us what we need. Apparently, the distribution channel is blocked."

Tony's mother used a lot of spices in her sauces, and oregano was one of her favorites. She probably used a lot of it. He wondered why they couldn't get through? Tony wanted to ask, but knew he shouldn't speak in the meeting. Maybe he could ask Jimmy later.

"Carlo." Dad used the same warning voice he

used when Tony was in trouble. He stared down the table with a strange expression on his face.

Carlo continued as if he hadn't spoken. "The question is, what can we do about it?"

"What about Oscar?" Titus asked. "We'll dress him up like a nurse."

Everyone laughed, but Carlo eyed Oscar up and down. "You know, it might work. How tall are you, Oscar, five-foot six or seven?"

"Five eight," Oscar mumbled, straightening a little.

"OK, so he's a little beefy for a girl, but I think it might work."

They all laughed again. What were they talking about? Why a nurse? It must be some kind of joke.

Tony smiled. Jimmy was definitely going to have to clue him in.

Oscar glowered, obviously unhappy. "You've got to be kidding. How would I do it?" He twirled the pen in his hand. "I can't exactly walk right in there and...ah..." he paused, flicking a glance at Tony, "demand oregano."

"Why not?"

Oscar placed the pen on the table, lining it up with the edge. "Don't you think it'll seem a little strange? Besides I have other responsibilities."

"I'll take care of them. In fact, I'll take care of everything. All you have to do is go and remove the impediment to our distribution."

Dad tried one more time, looking around the room. "Come on, guys. We can't do this. It could seriously hurt our business going forward."

No one spoke.

"Oscar," he said. "You don't want to do it, do

you?"

Oscar cleaned his nails and said nothing. No support for his dad coming from there.

Carlo glowered at Dad. "It's a calculated risk," Carlo purred. "We'll just have to finesse the supplier."

Dad jumped to his feet and pounded the table with his fist. Everyone jumped, including Tony. He'd never seen his father so mad. "Don't you understand? It will never work. We can't win this one."

Carlo's eyes narrowed into slits. "You'd better hope it works, Dominic." Menace laced his soft voice. "Because you have the most to lose. I would think you of all people would want to make sure it's flawless."

Dad slid back into his chair. "I understand."

Carlo nodded and turned away.

The meeting ended with Oscar planning to see the supplier, and everyone stood and left the room.

Tony followed, his head spinning. Why did Dad let Carlo talk to him like that? He should fire him.

And why didn't they just go to the store and buy some oregano until their supplier could get through? It was probably a lot more expensive, but it would work. No, it must be more than that. Maybe they needed way too much. He'd ask Dad later.

10

Peter left for Boulder the next morning. His appointment with Nora Lane, Cindy's best friend, was for eight o'clock before her first class. He arrived at the University of Colorado campus and, following her directions, found the coffee shop where they'd planned to meet.

The steamy aroma of espresso greeted him as he opened the glass doors and moved to the counter. Being early, he bought a cup of his favorite brew and stood back.

The place bustled with college students, some studying alone, some in groups, and many absorbed in their phones, waiting for service. Baristas behind the counter flew through the orders.

He stood in the crowded space, sipping his coffee until a table vacated and then pounced before anyone else could claim it.

A thin, brown-haired young woman, matching Nora's description, walked in right on time. She glanced his way, and he waved. After getting her coffee, she came over, introduced herself, and sat across from him. Swollen skin surrounded her dry, bloodshot eyes. "You got some ID?"

He flipped it out and showed her.

She nodded, and he put it back. He got right to the point. "You're aware Cindy was killed in a warehouse in Pinon Creek?"

She nodded again.

"I'm trying to find out why she was there." She didn't speak, so he went on. "Did she say anything to you?"

"No."

OK, that was short. "Her mom said she was at a charity event. Did she tell you about it?"

"A charity event?"

"Yes. Do you know what charity it was? Was she into any causes?"

"You mean besides the one that killed her?"

Peter folded his forearms on the table. "Do you know who killed her?"

Nora's brown-eyed gaze bored into him. "You killed her."

He jerked back, and his hands fell into his lap. "Pardon?"

Nora leaned forward. "The only thing she did for the past year was the DARE program you all sponsor. She was so involved she didn't have time for her friends." Her words spewed like lava, and tears ran down her cheeks, but she didn't brush them away.

"I never saw her anymore, and she skipped so many classes she was probably failing. What do you guys want, anyway?" She brought both hands up, wiping her tears and then pushing the bangs off her face. She held them for a moment and exhaled before letting them fall. "If you're after another convert to your cause, you can forget it. I told her she was nuts getting involved, but she wouldn't listen. Look where it got her—dead!" She cried harder, gulping in air.

He handed her a napkin and waited. He tried to make his voice gentle. "What do you mean it got her dead? How did the DARE program get her killed?"

"You...you policemen," she spat it out like she meant to say something derogatory. "You ask too much! She was a college student, and she shouldn't have been following dangerous criminals."

He sat upright, his heartbeat quickening. "What dangerous criminals? Who was she following?"

She glared straight into his eyes. "Don't play innocent with me. Are you expecting me to believe you guys weren't in on it? Like you didn't know what she was doing?"

How could he know what she was doing? He needed to ignore the frustration. "Listen, Ms. Lane, I have no idea what you're talking about. The DARE program is about prevention. It stands for Drug Abuse Resistance Education, and its primary mission is to provide kids with the information and skills they need to live drug-and-violence free lives." He was almost quoting their website, but he couldn't explain it better.

"That might be what the literature says, but it's not what you guys do. You ask people to do dangerous things—things they aren't trained to do."

What was she talking about? He placed both hands on the table and leaned in, skewering her with his gaze. "Not only would we not expect her to do anything dangerous, it would be illegal for her to involve herself in a police matter. So if she was following someone, we didn't know about or condone it. Now tell me, who was she following?"

Her eyes grew larger, and her jaw dropped at the force of his reaction. "I don't know." Some of the heat went out of her voice. "Cindy wouldn't tell me his name. She started acting stranger than usual and going to elementary schools to tell her story wasn't enough anymore. She hung around and followed people she thought looked suspicious. When I asked her about it, she told me she was"—she raised both hands and gestured air quotes—"working with the police"—she lowered her hands—"I tried to get her to give me a name, but she refused. I thought you guys told her not to tell me."

Peter remained silent.

"Remember when she helped get the dealer who supplied her brother before he died?" Nora asked.

He nodded.

"She got excited about it and decided to do more. She wanted to go higher up. She said they should know bringing drugs into Pinon Creek was a mistake, and it was too hot there to be worth it. So that's why she ended up in an abandoned warehouse. That's the only reason I can think of. She followed someone there, and they caught her." Nora stood. "I've got a class." She picked up her coffee and walked away.

Peter left the coffee shop and headed back to his car. First, what was Cindy doing following drug dealers? Second, how did she know they were dealers? And where did Mark fit in? Did he know what she was up to? He doubted it. Mark would never endanger a civilian.

Would he?

11

Robin woke with a terrible headache. Noting Mark was unchanged, she called a cab to take her home. Maggie couldn't complain about that. At least she wasn't alone.

"Any change?" Ed stood in the hall.

She shook her head and winced.

"Did you get any sleep last night?" Silvia called from the kitchen.

Robin and Ed moved into the kitchen, and she dropped into a chair, quickly regretting it as her head pounded. "Some, but not much I'm afraid."

"You look tired. Why don't you let us stay with Mark while you lie down? I'm worried about you."

Robin started to say no, but the day stretched out in front of her, long and exhausting, having to be upbeat when she felt lousy. She clamped her lips shut. She wasn't up to it. Besides, Mark's parents would call if there was any news. "I think I'll take you up on that. A good nap in my own bed sounds heavenly."

After eating some toast and eggs, she went upstairs, showered, and put on sweats. In the bedroom, she reached for the blinds.

An old blue sedan pulled up in front of the house, followed by two police cars. A tall man in a suit and a uniformed officer exited the sedan and marched up the walk before the police cars even came to a complete stop.

Robin hurried downstairs, went to the front door and opened it.

The tall man was about her father's age, his dark hair sprinkled with gray. There were crinkles next to his soft brown eyes, but he didn't smile. "Mrs. Clayton, my name is Isaiah Thompson. I'm with the Internal Affairs Division of the Colorado State Police." He handed her his badge. When she gave it back, he passed her a sheet of paper. "We have a warrant to search these premises."

She stared at the signature. Judge Lawson. Mark spoke of her with respect. The words blurred until she couldn't take them in.

He stepped forward, and she backed up to let him and a team of five men and two women enter.

"What's going on?" Ed came from the kitchen, a dishtowel in his hand.

"They have a search warrant."

"A warrant? What for? What is this about?"

Silvia followed her husband, and Ed's voice started to rise.

No one answered. They split up and moved through the house.

Robin knew most of them, some better than others, but she'd seen and said hello to all of them at some point. They either averted their gazes or watched her with sympathy as they slipped past, moving two by two, giving her a brief vision of Noah's Ark.

One stayed behind with Thompson, who faced her. "We're investigating the shooting your husband was involved in, and we'd like to ask you a few questions."

Involved in. Somehow, he made it sound as if

Mark had done the shooting instead of being shot.

"Of course." Robin gestured to the room behind her. "Come into the living room. Please sit. Can I get you anything?" How could her voice be so calm and polite when she was shaking inside? What did these people hope to find?

Thompson declined anything to drink and sat in one of the armchairs.

Silvia perched next to her husband on the couch.

Robin wished Mark were here.

The young officer brought out a notebook and pen and sat in a chair a little removed from the group, as if he wanted them to forget his presence.

When everyone settled, Thompson began, "As I'm sure you're aware, your husband was found in an abandoned warehouse the day before yesterday. Did he mention any business he may have had there at that time of the morning?"

Any ideas she'd had that he would be kind vanished. "No, he didn't." Where was this going?

"Do you know a woman named Cindy Carroll?"

"Yes, she's part of the DARE program." His silence made her want to continue. "Cindy had a personal tragedy involving drugs and wanted to help. She was killed in the warehouse, wasn't she?" The search resounded around her.

He slid some notes out of a leather folder. Two men went from the dining room into the kitchen and rattled through the cabinets. Two more men and two women climbed the stairs.

Was everything clean up there? In her rush to get down here, did she leave her underwear on the floor? She shook her head. What a dumb thing to worry about. Better concentrate.

"How well did your husband know her?"

"Reasonably well. They were all—"

"Were they having an affair? Is that how she ended up dead in an abandoned warehouse with your husband?"

Robin's mouth fell open. Shock kept her silent.

Not so her mother-in-law. "Now you wait a minute!" Silvia's face flared bright red as she sprang to her feet. "My son wouldn't do that to Robin."

Ed grabbed his wife's hand and tugged her down again, looking over to Robin. "Detective Thompson, we're finished answering questions without a lawyer present."

Robin shot him a grateful glance.

The officer folded his notebook and put it away. The detective opened and then closed his mouth as if he wanted to say more but knew from the note-taker's expression he wouldn't have support. It must be someone who liked Mark.

"Very well." Thompson stood. "When you're ready to answer questions about your husband's activities, give me a call. Until then I'll have to investigate on my own."

Before they could speak, an officer stuck his head in the doorway and cleared his throat. "Um, detective? We found something up here."

They followed the young officer and the detective up the stairs and into her bedroom. A briefcase lay open on the bed, money stacked inside. A lot of money. The bundles had hundreds on top.

Robin's hands grew slippery with sweat. "Where did you get that? It's not mine."

The detective scowled at her with a cross between scorn and pity. She must have imagined the pity, because if it did exist it disappeared fast. Hard distrust tightened his features. "Mrs. Clayton, do you recognize this case? It was found on the top shelf of your closet." He stepped back, revealing an old-fashioned black case with pushdown clasps.

She opened her mouth, but no words came. She cleared her throat and tried again. "No. I've never seen this before. I don't know how it got there."

A gloved officer closed the case, touching as little of it as possible, and clicked the latches with a pen. He picked it up by the sides and stowed it in a plastic bag.

Thompson gestured for her to precede him downstairs, and the search continued. The officers didn't seem to find anything else of interest.

When they finished, Thompson turned to her. "Mrs. Clayton, I would like to question you downtown regarding your husband's activities. I suggest you call your lawyer."

Robin changed into jeans and searched for the number of Susan Legrae, a legal secretary who went to her church. Susan promised to have someone meet her at the station. She went in the blue car with the note-taker and Thompson, her in-laws promising to follow in her car. They were silent the entire trip, allowing her to process what just happened. How long had the briefcase been in there? Being short, she didn't use the high shelf often, but it couldn't have been there long. Had Mark put it there? If so, why didn't he tell her? A sick feeling swirled in the pit of her stomach.

When they arrived at the station, she walked past the desk clerk without speaking. She'd been to the station often and always bantered with whoever was on desk duty.

This time, he looked at her and then down as if he

didn't know what to say.

That made two of them.

Thompson led her into an interview room, offered her some coffee, and left, closing the door behind him. Unlike the rooms on TV, with a long mirror on one wall, this resembled a regular conference room without any frills, just four once-white walls, ugly vinyl flooring, and a metal table and chairs.

Robin tried to relax. She had nothing to worry about, right? If one was innocent, one had nothing to worry about. So why did this fear curl in the pit of her stomach?

Where were Ed and Silvia? Were they being questioned? Hopefully her mother-in-law wouldn't get too upset. If they started questioning her about Mark, Silvia might not be able to control her temper.

Robin waited an eternity alone. The briefcase. She couldn't think of anything else. She put her face in her hands and pictured the people who came to search. Were there any bulges as if they had something under their clothes? The thought was just as ridiculous as Mark selling drugs or taking bribes.

A knock caused her to jump and hit her elbow on the table, sending a flash of pain up into her shoulder.

An older man pushed open the door and stepped through. He laid a brown leather briefcase on the table and smoothed back a lock of gray hair that fell onto his forehead.

Robin rubbed her arm, her gaze fixed on the briefcase, seeing instead a black one full of hundred-dollar bills lying on her bed. She clasped his outstretched hand.

"Mrs. Clayton, I'm Lester Grimes. You can call me Lester. Susan Legrae told me you needed some help."

He sat next to her. "Why don't you tell me what happened." His face was kind while he listened to her account. "Have you ever seen the briefcase before?"

"No. Mark's is brown like yours. Only his isn't as nice."

Lester smiled. "Have you a reason to believe Mark had that kind of money lying around?"

"No, of course not. We don't even have that kind of money in the bank, let alone in my closet."

"Have there been any strangers in your house?"

She frowned. "Not that I know of."

He wrote some notes. "Have you noticed Mark talking to people you've never seen before?"

Why would he ask that? She hesitated, but knowing he was on her side helped. "Not that I can recall."

"Is there anything else you think I should know?"

She pinned him with her gaze. "Mark is a good man and a good cop. He would never do what they're accusing him of."

Lester laid his hand over hers. "They don't know any more than you do." He patted her hand and released it. "They found some money in your house. So what? It isn't illegal to have money in your closet."

Robin gave him a small smile.

"Answer the questions they ask directly and try not to elaborate. He may attempt to goad you into an emotional outburst. Don't let him upset you. If I don't want you to answer, I'll place my hand on your arm, like this." He touched her forearm. "If you have a question for me, just lean over and whisper in my ear." He patted her arm. "It'll be OK."

She nodded, exhaling slowly. *Thank You, God, for sending help.*

He stepped out to let them know she was ready.

Thompson entered and sat in the chair across from her. He placed a small recorder and a file on the table, scooted the recorder to the middle, and switched it on. "This interview will be recorded."

She stared at it and said nothing. Her hands started to shake so she clasped them together under the table.

Thompson opened the file and removed a paper tablet. "Mrs. Clayton, did you know the deceased, Cindy Carroll?"

Why was he asking again? He'd asked already. "Yes, she was a young woman who helped out at the school in the DARE program."

He wrote on the tablet. "When was the last time you saw her?"

She lifted her gaze to the ceiling. "A couple months ago. I saw her at the mall."

He kept his focus on the tablet. "Did you stop and talk?"

What did that have to do with anything? "We said hello. She was coming in as I was leaving."

"What about your husband? When was the last time he saw her?"

"I don't know. I don't remember, but you might ask Peter."

Thompson braced his arms on the table. "So tell me about the briefcase. Did Mark tell you to hide it there?"

Ah-ha, here it comes. "I've never seen it before, and I don't know what it was doing up there."

"Do you and your husband share a closet?"

What a strange question. He must have seen Mark's closet across the room. "No, he has his own."

"And yet he chose to put it in your closet. Do you find that strange?"

Her lawyer touched her arm. She closed her mouth.

Thompson followed with another question. "Did you see Mark hide it there?"

Her frustration bubbled over. "Mark didn't hide anything. I told you I don't know how it got there!"

Lester put his hand on her shoulder as if to calm her. She took a breath and sat back in her chair, surprised she'd been sitting on its edge.

"Has your husband been acting strange? Maybe staying out later than usual?"

Where was he going with this? She twisted her hands before answering. "He's been working hard, if that's what you mean." Was that fear she heard in her voice? "Otherwise, no, he hasn't been acting strange."

"What about people he's been seeing? Have you seen him with anyone you don't know?"

She shook her head.

"Speak into the recorder please."

She faced the recorder. "Not that I know of. No."

Thompson leaned back and twirled his pen. "Have your husband's habits changed?"

"I don't know what you're getting at, but no, his habits haven't changed."

"Any major purchases? Like a car or other expensive item?"

Ah, so that's where he was going. "No, we haven't bought anything new for a while."

"The inside of your house is pretty fancy. We can tell if he's living above his means."

Lester had warned her about this. She gritted her teeth for a moment and then forced herself to relax. "I am an interior designer. My house needs to reflect my ability, and I purchased the things in it at designer's cost."

"We can look at your taxes, you know. We can have you and your husband audited if necessary. The IRS will love to know whether you've paid taxes on that money."

Her lawyer touched her arm. "Detective, I believe we're getting off the subject here."

Thompson exhaled. "Think about the last time you looked up in the closet. When was the last time you're sure the case wasn't there?"

Robin pictured the tiny space. "I painted my bedroom and closet a month or so ago. It wasn't there then."

"Is that the last time you looked up there?"

"That's the last time I can remember, yes."

He stared into her eyes.

She held his gaze.

"I believe you, Mrs. Clayton."

What? He believed her? Something in his face didn't make her feel better. In fact, she tensed. "You do?" It was a squeak. She cleared her throat again.

"Yes, I believe you didn't know about the briefcase."

She released her breath, but his manner kept her from lowering her guard.

Thompson lowered his gaze and wrote on the tablet. What would he write that wasn't on the recorder? She eyed the tablet but it was upside down. Plus, his handwriting was so bad, she couldn't have read it anyway. "I also believe you didn't know your husband was having an affair."

She jerked back and started to rise from her chair.

Lester grabbed her arm.

She sank into her seat, shaking. "My husband is not having an affair."

"Come on, Mrs. Clayton." His gaze softened as if with pity. "You know what infidelity looks like, don't you?"

Her mouth filled with saliva. She was going to be sick. Did he mean Carl, her lying, cheating ex-husband? How could he know about him?

Lester placed his arm around her shoulders. "Where are you going with this, detective?"

Thompson ignored him. "Why did you get divorced?"

"My ex-husband cheated on me with his secretary," Robin whispered.

Lester's arm stiffened, and he said nothing. Should she have told him? It simply hadn't occurred to her.

"Robin, the only person you call at that hour is your boyfriend." He talked slow and gentled his voice as if she wasn't too bright. "Cindy Carroll was in trouble, so she called her lover. Too bad he was in on it with them." He paused. The worst was coming.

She held her breath.

"That young woman called your husband for help, and he shot her."

Heat filled her face, and she wanted to scream at him to shut up. She was caught off balance, exactly as he intended. *Calm down*. But she couldn't. She felt like a blithering idiot.

Images flashed in her mind. Carl packing his clothes, saying he was the father of his assistant's baby. Her and Mark's repeated tries to get pregnant, and the cold hard realities of her miscarriages. Could it be true? Could he have gone to a younger woman looking to her for the family he wanted so badly? She must have lost whatever Lester said next, because when she came back to the conversation, he was telling her it was time to go.

Thompson smirked, knowing he'd scored.

Lester helped her stand on shaky legs, and she hobbled to where Ed and Silvia were waiting. Every muscle, held so rigid during the entire interview, now twitched. She wasn't sure how long her legs could support her.

"You did fine." Lester told her.

But it didn't feel that way. Why did she let Thompson get to her?

After taking one look at her face, Silvia shot up and guided her to a chair against the wall.

Robin rested her head on the wall and closed her eyes, putting all her effort into not throwing up.

Lester took her in-laws aside, their voices a blur.

She didn't try deciphering what they said. She wanted to get out of here—this station, where Mark loved working. She focused on Ed and stood. "Have you called the hospital?"

He put his arm around her as she stumbled. "Yes, but there's no change. Let's get you some lunch, and then we'll go."

Her watch said twelve twenty, but she wasn't hungry. They stopped in the hospital cafeteria, and she picked up a sandwich. Moving past the condiment stand, they found a table in a corner. Ed blessed the meal, and she took a bite. It tasted like paper, dry and sticking to her tongue. A gulp of water forced it down. Placing the sandwich back on her plate, she told them what the detective said.

"Well, he's just stupid then. One would think

someone of his rank would have a few more brain cells upstairs than that. I can't believe the police department would promote such an idiot."

Robin laughed over Silvia's vehemence, but before she knew what was happening, tears coursed down her cheeks. Not again. Then came the hiccups.

The cashier gave her a gentle smile, and some people nearby turned their way.

She rushed to the bathroom to splash cold water on her face.

When she got control, they finished lunch and hurried to Mark's room. The guard still sat outside the door, but now she viewed him less as a protector and more as a jailor. Either way, having someone guarding him would at least keep him safe.

Her heart warmed when she saw Peter sitting next to the bed trying to talk to Mark. Robin leaned over and kissed her husband's cheek. She sat in the chair next to Peter's and told him what happened. When they reached the part about the briefcase, he stiffened.

"How in the world did Mark get so much money? Did he say anything about a sting operation?"

"No, and wouldn't you have known about it if there was one?"

A funny look crinkled his face. "Yes, I suppose so. Unless the chief thought I was the leak."

"Mark would have been upset if that had been the case, and he would have told me. I'm sure Chief Donovan wouldn't have used Mark to trap you."

Peter's shoulders relaxed, and no one spoke.

Silvia pushed up from her chair and went into the restroom.

After she left, Ed broke the silence. "Peter, have you been investigating Cindy, and why she was in the warehouse with Mark?"

"You know she was working on the DARE program. But she was in a lot deeper. She thought she was helping the department by trying to discover the producer on her own. Apparently, she'd been following some pretty scary people around."

"Her little brother was killed about a year ago from an accident relating to drug use, wasn't he?" Robin asked.

"Yeah, he was ten. He somehow got hold of some cocaine, and he and his friends sniffed it. Then they climbed on the roof, convinced they could fly. He jumped first, flipped over, and landed on his back. They thought he was going to make it, but something happened, and he started bleeding internally. They stopped it. He died a couple days later. There was some speculation surrounding whether he had been given too much of a medication that induced the bleeding, but nothing was proven."

He resettled in his chair. "Cindy went kind of nuts. She found out who gave him the cocaine, and we arrested him. But we weren't able to go any higher. Someone told her about DARE, and she'd been traveling around telling her story in grade schools and middle schools since then." He crossed one leg over the other. "It seemed to be enough for a while but apparently not anymore. Mark and I had no idea she was following someone. If we had, we would've made her stop."

"I don't think you could have changed her mind." Ed shook his head. "It sounds like she was obsessed."

Peter's eyelids drooped. "I wish now I'd talked to her about becoming a cop. At least if she was determined to do police work, she would've been trained. Maybe she'd still be here."

"Detective Thompson accused Mark of having an affair with her," Robin blurted, studying Peter's face.

His foot thumped to the floor, and he sat up straight. "Of course he wasn't! You don't believe such nonsense, do you? Mark wouldn't do that to you. He has better values. The chief wouldn't have said it either." He stopped for a breath, understanding crossing his face as he gave a quick nod. "Detective Thompson was trying to get a rise out of you." He swallowed. "IA does that."

"He certainly got a rise out of Silvia back at the house." She chuckled. "I thought she was going to slap him. I think she would've if Ed hadn't stopped her. Now, it's kind of funny, but at the time, I was afraid she would get herself arrested."

Both Ed and Peter laughed. "I thought so, too," Ed said. "I saw myself bailing her out for assaulting a police officer. I wouldn't blame her. I wanted to slug him, too."

"I wish I'd said something," Robin whispered. "I let him run over me like a train in that interview room, and I didn't fight back."

Peter sat back and looked her in the eye. His gaze was like a laser. "Trust me, Robin. You don't win by fighting in a police interview, especially with Internal Affairs. You did the right thing."

"When he said Mark shot Cindy, I freaked out. I had no idea they were trying to pin murder on him. What about the fact he was shot, too? I should have asked how he thought that happened."

Peter crossed his legs again. "He wouldn't have answered. Like I said, he was trying to get a rise out of you. He wanted somewhere to take the investigation.

You didn't give it to him. From what I hear, it sounds like you did great."

It didn't feel great. It felt as if she'd let Mark down, as if she'd failed to defend him when he couldn't defend himself. But how would she explain the money? First, the two thousand dollars in his pocket, and now however much was in the briefcase. Was it possible the police planted it? It didn't seem possible, but neither did the other explanations.

Her face burned over what the detective said. One thing was true though. She knew what infidelity looked like, and it didn't look like Mark. Did it? Robin tried to compare Carl's behavior with Mark's. Was there any similarity? No. Mark worked late, but he called to let her know. And when she called him, he was always where he was supposed to be.

Carl would expect her to believe the most ridiculous things. She pretended at first, but down deep, she knew he was lying. She searched her heart. Did she ever feel Mark was dishonest? In the beginning of their relationship, she believed everything was a lie, so she was tough on him. But after a while, she began to believe in him. Would this break her trust?

12

Peter headed to the station. If Internal Affairs searched Mark's house, they must have thought they had something on him before they found the money in his closet. The money in his pockets would've been suspicious enough, but wasn't it overkill? He wouldn't have been carrying it around. He would have left it with the rest of the money.

Did IA think he was paying someone off? That didn't make much sense because it wasn't enough money for a payoff. It seemed as though someone wanted to tease Internal Affairs. As if they wanted to ensure a search of Mark's house. If so, then they must have known there'd be something to find.

If Mark was guilty of a bribe, then he wouldn't have shown up at the drop unless he was there to either distract or kill Cindy. If that were the case, they wouldn't have shot him, would they? Why would they shoot their protector? One thing he knew: if IA believed Mark was the leak, they would concentrate on him to prove their case.

In his gut, he felt Mark was innocent, but how could he prove it? He needed to know what IA was thinking. He settled at his desk. Libby's picture smiled out at him from the frame on the corner. His World's Greatest Dad coffee mug sat unwashed since he'd gotten the call about Mark. He needed to clean it out, but first he had to call his contact at the lab.

"Hey, Bob. It's Peter. I know this is a lot to ask, but I need a favor."

"Is this about Mark Clayton?" The voice sounded far away.

"Yeah, can you give me any information on his investigation?"

"First of all, how is he? Is he awake yet?"

How much did Bob know? "No, but he's stable, so we're hoping it'll be soon. I'm trying to keep him from getting railroaded before he even has a chance to wake up and defend himself. Is there anything you can tell me?" Interfering in an Internal Affairs' investigation could cost Peter his job, but Mark was worth it.

"I don't know much because I'm not working this case. I heard they've zeroed in on Mark, and they don't want to hear anything else."

Oh, great, just what he thought.

Bob huffed. "Let me pull it up. It looks like we did the autopsy on Ms. Carroll right away because of the officer involvement. I don't think there's much on this report you don't already know. A blonde female shot in the chest with a 9mm at close range. Is that what Mark carried?"

"Yeah, but the gun at the scene wasn't the one he usually carries. That one's missing."

"Ah. Ballistics hasn't come in yet. Was his police issue gun found at home?"

"No."

"Hmm."

Peter wondered what Bob was thinking. Why would Mark have another gun? They must have planted it on him. He hadn't reported his gun stolen, and Peter was sure he would have. It was a pretty serious oversight.

"The angle of the exit wound is slightly up from the entrance wound, so your shooter is most likely shorter than your victim." Bob went on. "Mark is how tall?"

"About six feet."

"It says here Cindy was five eleven without shoes, so she would be about six with tennis shoes on. But that isn't enough to clear him on its own."

"What about being shot from below, like from the main floor to a mezzanine?" From the blood spray that didn't happen, but he wanted Bob to say it.

"No, the trajectory wasn't steep enough, and gunshot residue on the victim suggests the shooter was within three to five feet of the victim."

"What about Mark's clothes? Can you tell if he discharged his weapon?"

"No, I don't have anything here except the autopsy file. They're locking this down, so I don't think I'll be able to help much. If I hear something I think will help you, I'll give you a call. I liked Mark."

Peter hung up and sat back. Liked, he'd said. As if Mark were already dead. The room was empty, so he pulled out the notes he'd started on everyone in the unit. He and Mark had been best friends too long for him to be involved in something Peter didn't know about. He would not consider him a suspect. There had to be another option.

Before he could begin, Officer Daniels approached and dropped a file on his desk. "I got the names and addresses you asked for from the dinner the other night. Turns out it wasn't a charity event; it was a senate fundraiser."

"Oh? Which one?"

"Senator Allen."

"Anybody interesting on the guest list?"

"Depends on what you call interesting. The mayor's on it, which is reasonable since it's his party, but I didn't see Donovan's name." He grinned. "I wonder how he wriggled out of it this time."

Peter shrugged. "Knowing how much he hates these things, maybe the mayor gives him a pass now and then. Before you go, what did you find on the number I gave you from Robin's phone?"

"You were right. It was a throwaway."

"Pretty much what I expected." He pinched his lip between two fingers then pulled his hand away. "Do we have any news on the green sedan?"

Daniels shook his head. "Nothing so far. Our garages haven't seen it, but if he drove it down to Denver, we may never find it."

"Let's get someone calling all the places they can find in Louisville, Lafayette, Boulder, and as much of Denver Metro as you can. Have them ask if they've seen a green sedan with damage to the front left side. It would've been yesterday or today, so they should remember. Or it could still come in this week."

When Daniels nodded and left, Peter scanned the list. Pinon Creek was still small enough that the Sky Lake Hotel was the only place suitable to host an event of any size, so this had to be it.

The mayor was there all right, along with many city leaders and the more influential members of Pinon Creek society, as well as some other names Peter recognized—Carlo Litzi and Dominic Rossetti.

Peter grinned. They might be worth a closer look.

13

Before starting his shift, Tony ran upstairs to see if his father needed anything. If so, maybe he could get out of clearing tables. The door was closed, so now he had no choice. He huffed and started back down the hall. He had just swung around the corner to the stairs when the door clicked open and Carlo bellowed.

"Dominic, it has already been decided. I know you don't like it, but that's too bad. And if you don't see to it, I will."

Tony sprinted down the stairs before Carlo or his dad caught him listening. What was that about? And why did Dad put up with Carlo's attitude?

He slowed his pace through the dining room. If he took Jimmy's place in the fall, it would mean working for Carlo. Ugh. Maybe it would work out, but judging from what had just happened, his dad wouldn't be any help if Carlo became nasty. He passed the hostess stand and smiled at his mom. Maybe he should learn to cook.

As he dodged the occupied tables in the dining room, his cell phone rang. Uh-oh, he forgot to turn it on vibrate. He fumbled it out of his pocket to shut off the ring. Sure enough, his mother heard it and shot him the evil eye. Lucy's image grinned from the screen. He hurried into the kitchen, where his mom couldn't see, and answered.

"Hi, Tony. How're you doing?"

Better since she was calling. "Good, clearing tables."

"Oh, I'm sorry. I didn't get you in trouble, did I?"

He wouldn't care if she did. "No, don't worry. It's fine. What's up?"

"Do you remember the guy who taught youth group last week, Mark Clayton?"

"Yeah, he was good. You know, down-to-earth, not so religious." Ugh, why did he say that? He hoped she knew what he meant.

"Yeah, I like him, too. Anyway, he's a policeman, and he was shot in the line of duty."

Did he hear her right? "Shot? Is he OK?"

"The doctors think so, but for now he's still unconscious. His wife, Robin, is a good friend of my family, and we're going to the hospital to visit tomorrow. Do you want to come?"

Did he want to come? Was the Pope Catholic? "Yeah, sure. What time?"

"How about four o'clock, after school? We don't have to stay long, but I want Robin to know we care."

"Hey, I hope he gets better. I'll pick you up at four."

When he hung up, Tony shot his fist in the air. Yes! Lucy was beginning to like him. Really like him. Maybe even enough to go out with him on a real date. Lunches after church at her house were fun and all, but it would be great to be alone with her and just talk. He turned his phone to silent and shoved it in his back pocket. Just in time, too. His mom came around the corner.

When she saw him, she smiled. "You look happy. What happened?"

"What? Can't a guy be happy?"

She ruffled his hair and handed him an apron. "Would this happen to be about a cute little brunette?"

Tony slipped the apron over his head and tied it in back. "Maybe...hey, I need the night off tomorrow. Is that OK?"

"Yeah, you know I have a sweet spot for romance." She swatted him on the rear as she passed by. "Don't be out too late."

He got the bus tub and moved to the first table. It had never taken him this long to ask a girl out. Something about her was different, though, and it was clear from the start that if he didn't handle it right, he wouldn't get another chance. An invitation to lunch with her family had taken weeks. *Take it slow. Don't blow it.*

He cleared the first table and wiped it off, moving to the kitchen to unload. He tried to put Lucy out of his mind and concentrate on his job, but his grin kept returning. Visiting sick people wasn't his idea of a date, but since it meant seeing Lucy again, it would be worth it. And Mark was a good guy, he didn't deserve something like this. Tony cleared and wiped down several tables.

His mom came by, squeezed his shoulders, and kissed him on the cheek. "Two of our servers called in sick, and I'll need you to help out."

"What if someone wants alcohol?"

"Gina will circulate with the drinks tray. Thankfully, it's not Friday or Saturday night. Tell them she'll be by to take their drinks order." She started to move around him and stopped. "Hey, do you think Lucy would like to help? We have a ten-top reserved and an eight-top at the same time."

"Can she?" Without waiting for a response, he pulled out his cell phone and hit a speed dial button. "I'll ask."

Lucy answered on the first ring, her voice making him smile. "Mom says we're shorthanded at the restaurant, and she wants to know if you would like to help serve."

She hesitated.

His palms began to sweat.

"Now?"

"Yeah. Sorry for the late notice." He added, "You'll get paid, and you get tips."

"Sounds fun, and I can use the money. I'll be right over."

He ran into the kitchen and changed from a black apron, to a white one with big pockets in the front. He grabbed an order pad and some pens and started taking orders, watching the door for Lucy. This would be her first time at the restaurant. Would she like his parents?

"Excuse me, young man," a gentle voice intruded. "I asked about the ravioli."

"Oh!" He blinked and focused on the table before him, pasting a quick smile in place as he answered the gray-haired woman. "The ravioli is homemade, and the filling is a choice of either beef or a four-cheese blend."

His parents were nothing like hers.

"Ooh, that sounds good. I'll have the cheese."

The man with her nodded. "Yes, I'll have the same." He closed his menu and handed it over. "And some bread please."

Tony jotted their orders, pen poised, patiently waiting while the lady made up her mind about the dressing on her salad.

Sometimes his mother cursed in the kitchen. What if Lucy heard her? He'd have to keep her in the dining room.

He was back by the computer entering an order when Lucy arrived. Her beautiful, long brown hair swung past as his mother hustled her off. He bit his lip. So much for keeping her out of the kitchen. Oh, well, nothing he could do about it now.

It turned out to be so busy, he didn't even think about her. Or his mother. By the time he slowed, only a few customers remained. His mom came over with a smile.

"OK, guys, I can cut you loose now. Gina and Mike can handle the rest." She handed them their wages and tips and turned to Lucy. "Thank you so much. I don't know what I would have done tonight without you and Tony."

Lucy shoved the wad of bills into her pocket with a grin. "Wow. Thanks, Mrs. Rossetti. This was great. Anytime you need someone to fill in, give me a call."

His mother's smile was huge.

Tony grinned. Mom liked Lucy, he could tell. "You guys take some dessert home with you."

Tony folded his money in his wallet and took Lucy to the kitchen to pick out a dessert. Although it was late, they decided to go back to his house to eat.

He let her in the front door, and she gazed around the large entry, bending to take off her shoes. He kicked his off near hers and showed her to the kitchen.

She scanned the black granite countertops and tipped her head to the pendant lights and stainless appliances. Then she ran her hand over the white marble island and perched on a barstool. "Wow, this is beautiful. Your mom has great taste."

Tony glanced around, but his gaze bounced right back to Lucy. She was way better to look at than a dumb old kitchen. He probably shouldn't say so though. "Mom sometimes experiments in here, so she wanted a nice space."

He dropped the tiramisu on the island and went to get plates and silverware.

Lucy lifted the cover off the to-go box. "You're so lucky. I never get food like this."

"Believe it or not, neither do I. You tend not to want it so much when you clean it off people's plates all day."

She laughed.

He placed her piece on a plate and pushed it over. "So is your whole family going tomorrow?" Maybe if he got her to talk about them, he'd find out if they liked him.

She picked up her fork. "My mom's going, and my brothers. Dad has to work."

Tony set his piece on a plate and pushed it over next to hers. It would be easier if her dad wasn't there. Her mom liked him, but he felt uncomfortable around her dad. Her brothers were bad enough. They were nice to him, but he wasn't sure they wanted him dating their sister.

He and Lucy laughed and talked, and ate their desserts. Afterward, he walked her down the driveway and opened her car door. Strange how he wanted to do these small courtesies for her that he used to think were corny.

She gave him a quick kiss on the cheek and slid into her car.

He watched her turn the corner before heading

inside. When he strolled in the door, he tried to visualize it from her perspective—the flowers in the entry, the polished furniture in the living room, the wide staircase. Her whole house could fit in two of these rooms, but hers felt warm and cozy. Given the chance, he'd rather live there than this giant place.

He mounted the stairs two at a time and entered his bathroom. Even here, the differences were obvious. Marble gleamed on every surface, but it was cold. He began brushing his teeth. Her family was so cool. Too bad his couldn't be more like hers. They actually seemed to like each other. Like Grandma Katherine. She went to church and made him pray before meals and stuff.

He climbed into bed and stared up at the ceiling. After almost forgetting to pray that first lunch at Lucy's house, he'd remembered. It was a good thing, too, because her brothers were watching. They were Christians, and they believed all the stuff about God and Jesus saving your soul and all that. Sometimes he wished he believed in something. He turned over. Grandma would like Lucy. Maybe they could visit her sometime. But Lucy wouldn't want to go out with him anymore if she knew what his family was really like.

14

Robin gripped her coffee cup with one hand and flipped past hangers with the other. Today was Cindy Carroll's funeral. She chose a black rayon dress and trudged into her bathroom to shower. Was it a good idea to go? She didn't know Cindy well, but she felt she had to pay her respects. If he were awake, Mark would be going and taking her. The zing Agent Thompson had launched her way sizzled in her head. There was no way Mark was having an affair, but she had to know more about this woman.

"They're having a small service for Cindy tomorrow," Libby had said. "Why don't you come with Tori and me? Three sets of ears are better than two. If we get people talking about her, maybe we can find out what she was like, how she ended up in the warehouse, and why she was with Mark."

It sounded good yesterday, but now, facing it, it seemed crazy. What if Cindy's family thought Mark was responsible in some way for her death? Would they shun her, maybe even kick her out? She scowled at the mirror as she brushed her teeth. It didn't matter. She had to try.

She headed downstairs to the kitchen for some breakfast. Libby would be here in fifteen minutes.

Libby picked her up, and they sped to the church. They didn't even try to turn in to the full lot. Instead,

Libby drove around the tree-lined streets, searching for a place to park. She ended up two streets away, in front of a tan house with red shutters.

Robin got out of the car and breathed in the cool scent of the crab apple tree blooming in the yard. She tried to calm the flutter in her stomach as they walked to the church. An old-fashioned steeple with a cross on top towered over the average-sized white church. They threaded their way up the broad steps, through the crowd at the front door, and entered.

With a balcony hidden under high vaulted ceilings, it was tough to know how many the church held, but the ample pine pews in the sanctuary were full. Already people were standing in the aisles, and a line formed along the back for those who would have to stand.

"This is a small service?" Robin whispered.

"I'm surprised, too. I didn't know so many people knew her." Libby lifted onto her toes then jostled her way to the middle section.

Robin craned her neck, seeing around Libby's head to where another Libby waved to them. Uncanny how alike the twins were. Robin never could tell them apart, but since she seldom saw Tori, it didn't matter. She followed Libby through the throng to the saved seats, trying to keep from stepping on anyone.

Peter and Greg were there with the chief, but Libby didn't stop to talk. She just waved and moved forward to sit with her sister.

The minister spoke of faith and passion—faith in God and passion in life. He said Cindy carried a passion for getting drugs off the street and away from kids. "She gave her life," he said, "in the pursuit of this noble cause."

Libby tapped Robin's hand and nudged her toward the aisle.

The service had concluded. Grabbing her purse, she slid along the pew and joined the flow heading outside.

People milled around expressing their condolences to the family.

Libby and Tori skirted the line and approached an older woman waiting at the door.

"Did you get a key?" Libby asked.

The woman held up a small ring with two keys on it. "I have my own for when Virginia goes on vacation."

"Good, we'll meet you there."

Stepping around a bed of daffodils, Robin hurried to keep up with Libby as she strode across the grass. For a small woman, she really moved. "Where are we going?"

Libby fished car keys from her purse. "We're setting food out at Virginia's for the reception."

"Oh." Robin trailed her to the car. At least this would make her feel better about crashing the funeral.

They drove to Mrs. Carroll's house and unloaded coolers from both Libby's and Tori's trunks.

Other people arrived on the same errand, and soon, enticing food arranged buffet-style, heaped two long tables while extras crammed the counters.

Mrs. Carroll arrived minutes later. Her eyes grew large. Then she blinked rapidly. Had they made her cry again? "I was going to have a meat and vegetable tray or something." Her lips trembled then pressed into a thin line. "I hadn't even thought about what people were going to eat. Thank you so much."

Robin stared at her feet. She hadn't thought to

bring anything, let alone the amount of food Libby unloaded from her trunk. Did everyone make something but her? She hurried to help Libby and Tori arrange their offerings so no one would know she had arrived empty-handed.

The three of them took turns serving at the buffet and mingling with the guests, trying to understand Cindy. Stories about her sense of humor and her zest for life filled the house. Having experienced death in their family when their parents died, Libby and Tori said talking about the loved one was good for the grieving process.

Robin watched Tori speak to a family member and tried to copy her, encouraging friends to talk. Hopefully, one of them could uncover why she might have been in the warehouse with Mark.

A blond young man resembling Cindy stood in a small group of students.

Robin hovered at the edge with a drinks tray.

"She was so stubborn sometimes, but she was fearless," he said. "One time she and Mom had been shopping all day, and when she dropped Mom off, she stopped in for a glass of water. The rest of us were gone somewhere, and the house was quiet. Mom entered first and froze."

Robin leaned in closer.

He chuckled. "Cindy tripped over her, and when she stood up, she saw a man in a mask in the living room with the computer pulled out and all but one cord disconnected. He hesitated, not knowing what to do. He must have thought they'd be out longer or something. Cindy screamed, 'Get out of here!' and stomped her foot."

Everyone, including Robin, laughed.

"The guy dropped the computer and ran past them and out the door. Mom said Cindy was so mad, she was surprised the guy didn't get a kick in the pants on his way out."

The group laughed again, and one by one, they spoke of the Cindy they knew. Some were crying, some were laughing, but everyone had a story.

When the conversation lagged, Robin led them over to a table laden with gooey desserts, and their eyes lit up.

"You know, it would be in complete character for her to be in the warehouse, but not for the reason the moron policeman suggested," a woman spoke.

Oh, good. Finally.

"I can't believe he thought she was mixed up in it. It makes me furious. She hated drugs. She was on such a mission. She wouldn't have stopped until all illegal drugs were wiped out of Pinon Creek. I wish she'd lived to see her dream come true." The woman's voice broke and she sniffled.

One of the guys reached over to hold her. Most of the rest were wiping their eyes.

Another guy, Brandon, Robin thought that was his name, said, "Hey, remember the time she got all upset about the veterinary program?"

Some nodded with smiles.

He spoke to the ones who had blank looks. "We started taking vet classes because we thought we wanted to help animals. Then we found out they were using healthy animals to practice surgeries and putting them to sleep afterward. The college tried to tell her it didn't matter because they took them from the shelters and they were going to die anyway." He rolled his eyes and turned to a couple of the other guys. "Remember when she dragged us to a protest, and we marched for three days?"

"You bet!" the tallest one shouted. "I still have the calluses."

Others laughed and murmured.

"She got us all on TV, and the dean made a huge mistake," the crying woman said. "He told her she couldn't learn to operate on dead tissue. So she said, 'What are you telling me? That students learning to be surgeons in medical school operate on healthy people and then kill them afterward?' I thought I was going to die laughing at the expression on old Grimshaw's face when she said that. And on TV!"

"Well, don't keep us in suspense, what happened?" one of the brunettes, maybe Laurie, said.

"Yeah, what happened?" Robin said.

Brandon faced her. "Some of the teachers agreed and asked permission to open a small vet practice to help animals instead of killing them. Most had never felt right about it. Grimshaw approved it, and now the school has one."

About three hours later, after cleaning everything, Libby was ready to take Robin home. They hugged Mrs. Carroll good-bye, and Robin felt about as low as she could remember. This girl, who defended causes, died defending the one she believed in most. She must have been a remarkable person. And here Robin was, only here to protect her reputation. Well, and Mark's. She'd do anything to protect Mark.

Knowing Cindy's life was cut short when her life, which meant so little, went on...Well, Someone upstairs must have messed up. What would she have done, had something similar happened to her? Probably curl up in a corner and hide. She certainly wouldn't have charged after them as Cindy had.

Libby unlocked the doors, and Robin climbed into her car. No way should such an admirable young woman have died for nothing. The people who did this would have to pay. They had to be stopped.

But what could she do?

Libby turned in her seat and eyed her before starting the engine. "Did you find out anything?"

"I can't say I uncovered anything helpful."

Libby pulled away from the curb. "I know. Me either. It's not like her friends are going to say anything negative about her at her funeral, but she was an exceptional person, wasn't she? Who would want to kill her?"

"Aren't we assuming the drug dealers did?"

"Yeah, I guess so. It's the only thing she had in common with Mark."

Robin glanced at Libby's profile. "The police suggested she might be having an affair with him."

Libby turned the corner into the hospital parking lot. "You can't even think for a minute he'd do something like that, Robin, for heaven's sake."

Chastised, Robin decided to change the subject. "Did you hear the guy say something about first Joey, now her? Do you think she might have found out something more about how Joey got the drugs that killed him?"

"After hearing about her, I think it's entirely possible. Maybe if we find out more about her little brother, we can find out what Cindy was thinking when she went to the warehouse."

"We also need to find out why Mark was with her. Did he meet her there or was he following up on something and he didn't expect her?"

Libby glided to the curb, and Robin reached for the door handle. She turned. "You know, we've all been thinking Mark may have suspected someone in the department, but what if Cindy suspected someone? Do you think something she told him made him afraid to contact dispatch?"

Libby paused, her hand on the gearshift. "Could be, but why wouldn't he confide in Peter? He knew Peter would die for him. Why didn't he trust him?" Hurt tightened Libby's voice.

"He did trust him, Libby, I know he did. There's another reason." She paused for a second. "Maybe we should concentrate on Joey. Can you talk to Peter? Maybe find out what happened?"

"Yeah, I guess. At least it's a place to start."

Robin thanked Libby for the ride, slid from her seat, and hurried inside. She checked her phone again. No messages from Mark's parents. She didn't know if that was a good sign or a bad one.

She raced to the elevator, desperate now to see her husband. Mrs. Carroll said Chief Donovan was such a nice man and even visited Joey in the hospital.

Joey had taken quite a shine to him. Apparently, the day he died, he'd wanted to talk to the chief, and Cindy told him Chief Donovan would be visiting later that evening. He was dead before Donovan got the chance. What if Joey knew something? His mother didn't seem upset about it. No one thought it important. Maybe it wasn't. But what if it was? What if Joey told someone else? Someone he thought he could trust, like a policeman? Like one of Mark's friends?

15

Tony checked his watch again. The teacher droned on. If he didn't leave soon, he wouldn't be able to run home. Finally, the bell rang, and he flew out to his car. No time to go to his locker, he'd have to get his homework after.

Bright sunlight blinded him as he hit the double doors. Sliding into his car, he put on his sunglasses and raced out of the parking lot. Mom usually went home between the lunch rush and dinner. Maybe he could catch her there.

At the top of the stairs, he glanced into his parents' room—no one there. He raced to the kitchen—vacant, too. He'd hoped to ask her if he should buy flowers for Mark. Mom never showed up at the hospital empty-handed, but did you buy flowers for guys? It seemed kinda weird.

He plucked an apple out of the dish on the counter and munched on it as he drove to the restaurant. He pulled around, went through the back door and down the hall. The scent of freshly baked bread drifted his way long before he reached the loaded racks. He breathed in the garlic fragrance of Mom's famous sauce and the spicy scent of sausage. His stomach growled. The apple wasn't cutting his hunger. He grabbed a small loaf of bread off the top rack and tore off a hunk.

Mom stood at the other side of the kitchen in the

middle of a meeting. The sous chef, the line cooks, and the prep cooks surrounded her, faces intent as they nodded at her directions.

A man shoving a dolly loaded with produce boxes asked him to move aside.

He stepped into the kitchen to let him pass. This was a bad idea. She would want to know who Mark was and why Tony wanted to go, or worse come up with something for him to do.

He'd ask Lucy about the flowers. He pivoted and tiptoed back out. She'd know…all women knew these things, right? It was communicated to them at birth or something. Anyway, if he got stopped now, he'd be late picking her up. Not happening.

He slipped behind the shelves and down the hall again. As he opened the back door, Carlo's voice echoed into the hallway. He stuck his head around the door. Carlo and that Oscar guy from the meeting walked near the dumpsters and stood talking. He didn't want Carlo to see him, so he waited. Maybe they'd move on. But if they didn't, he either had to go to the kitchen, and risk his mother giving him a job to do or pass Carlo and hear a bunch of insults.

Insults were better than being late today of all days. He took a step forward.

"Take this now." Carlo handed Oscar a small packet. "When it's time to move, I'll call. You'll get the other half after." They moved away from the dumpsters and around the building toward the parking lot.

Tony heaved a chest full of dumpster air, and coughing, sprinted to his car. If he didn't hurry, he'd still be late.

Lucy stood waiting on her porch, and her mother

and brothers weren't with her. She came across her lawn as he got out. "It's just us. Mom and the guys are going later."

He opened her door and closed her inside, running back around to his side. The car growled to life. He loved that sound.

"So how well do you know Mark?"

She shifted in her seat. "He and Robin volunteer at some of the same things my parents do. Mostly youth stuff, you know, the mission trip last year and the passion play. And he coaches my brothers' summer softball team. So we know them pretty well." He glanced over, and she grinned. "How about you?"

Did her eyes always have that sparkle? He turned his gaze back to the road. "I just know him from Sunday school. But I like him a lot."

He drove in silence for a few blocks and then stole another glance at her. She was staring out the window. "I can't believe how nice it is out today," he said. "The snow we had is completely gone." *OK, moron, is that all you can think of, the weather?*

"Yeah, it's beautiful out."

The silence lengthened. The hospital loomed ahead. He found a space to park and hopped out, hurrying to open her door.

Sure enough, once inside, Lucy led the way straight to the gift shop and made a beeline to the ferns. He almost laughed. A plant was the perfect gift for a guy. Why didn't he think of it? He pulled out his wallet, and her eyes sparkled again as she handed it over. "My mom said he's in Room 413."

The earthy smell of the plant in his hands didn't quite cover the antiseptic tang in the air. They stepped into the elevator. Tony pushed four and scowled at the gleaming elevator numbers. He should say something witty. Something to make her laugh. Or at least something to make her think he cared about the cop. Or...well, anything! Between last night and today, they'd never been alone this long. Usually her rowdy brothers kept the conversation interesting. By now, she probably thought he was a complete dweeb.

The doors opened, and they filed out. Lucy paused to read the wall sign then veered right toward 413. He tried not to look into any of the occupied rooms along the hall. It was easy to see which one was Mark's—a police officer sat in the hall outside. He wrote their names on a clipboard along with the time.

Robin stood when she saw them and hustled over. "Lucy, come on in." She gave Lucy a hug and then took the plant from him. "Tony, it's good to see you. Thank you for the gift. It's lovely." She held the plant with one hand and gave him a side hug with the other.

Man, these church people sure were huggers. Tony couldn't remember getting hugged this much except from Grandma. But then she was a church person, too. Maybe this was how they all behaved.

Robin ushered them to a couple of chairs.

Tony focused on Robin, trying not to stare at Mark. He looked the same except for the white bandage on his head and the wires sticking out of his gown. He lay there like a statue. An older couple sat across from him—must be Mark's parents. Some women hovered, too. Low conversation surrounded him. Robin looked upset. Had she gotten bad news from the doctor? She tried hard to be upbeat, but tension vibrated in the room.

Lucy must have felt it, too, because she stood up. After smiling and shaking everyone's hand, he followed her out.

Crisp outdoor air eased the hospital smells from his lungs. He opened Lucy's door then hurried to climb in himself.

She turned to him as he buckled his seatbelt. "Do you think he's OK? Robin seemed pretty worried."

"I thought so, too. But I don't know her as well as you do, so I didn't want to say anything. He looked good though, like he was sleeping."

"I know. I had the urge to shake him."

He pulled out of the parking lot, careful not to squeal his tires. Something told him it wouldn't impress her. "I wonder what happened. They don't know yet do they?"

"No. Mom says they're hoping to find out more when he wakes up."

"Robin's a cool person though, isn't she?" he asked, realizing he liked her. "She matches Mark."

Lucy grinned. "I know what you mean. They're good together, and I like her. Listen, I'll be going to the hospital fairly often if you want to come sometimes."

"OK." He swallowed a grin and focused on the green light. "Let me know next time, and I'll see if I can come."

He hoped she would call tomorrow.

16

After the funeral, Peter returned to the station and picked up the list of people who'd attended the campaign dinner. Hmm, Dominic Rossetti and Carlo Litzi. He'd love it if they were involved. Something was off about them. Nothing was ever proven, of course, but they'd been suspects a few times. He glanced up as Greg and David entered.

David grabbed his keys out of his drawer and left again.

Greg sat at his desk.

Peter sauntered over. "Perfect timing. Care to take a trip with me?"

"Sure, are you going to the hospital?" Greg pushed back his chair.

"No, but it involves a great Italian restaurant."

Greg's eyes narrowed. "I know it can't be lunch because I saw what you ate after the funeral." He tapped his fingers on the armrest. "What have you got?"

Peter handed over the pages. "Look who went to the campaign dinner Thursday night."

Greg skimmed the list. "Ah, Rossetti and Litzi, eh? I'd love to catch them at something. That Carlo creep just screams sleazy, and the I-know-something-you-don't look on his face makes me want to punch him."

Peter laughed. "I didn't know you had such

violent tendencies."

Greg followed him out. "Only when it comes to his kind. You know…the cocky type."

Peter pulled into Rossetti's parking lot. The location—high on a hill overlooking Pinon Creek, surrounded by pine, blue spruce, and aspen trees—was outstanding. Beautifully landscaped, the property alone must be worth a few million.

"Look at this place." He slid out of the car. "Libby and I've been landscaping our backyard. The blue spruce and bristlecone pines near the entrance are worth a fortune. They might be indigenous to the area, but bristlecones are pricey."

Greg joined him, and they sauntered to the edge of the parking lot, taking in the vista before them. "What a view. They spared no expense building this place. Wonder what their bank loan is?"

"I can't imagine." Shaking his head, Peter led the way to the entrance.

A quiet aura of elegance greeted them. Big windows framed the mountain's natural beauty on one side and the city of Pinon Creek on the other. During the day, one requested a table with a mountain view, but at night, the city lights offered a fantastic vista. A large bar nestled into the left side of the grand space, and a graceful staircase curved to the second floor.

They paused inside the door.

Peter kept his voice low. "I've done some checking, and both the land and the restaurant are owned by Dominic and Maria Rossetti."

Greg whistled, still keeping it low so as not to draw attention. "I've never thought about it before, but a lot of money's tied up here. The question is does it all come from the food or is something else going on?"

They stopped at the host stand.

The tantalizing aroma of tomatoes and Italian sausage drifted out of the kitchen. Despite the ebbing lunch rush, the dining room remained about half full, the low murmur of conversation underplaying the soft, crooning music. "I can tell you at dinner it can be tough to get a reservation."

The hostess glanced up with a smile and asked if she could get them a table. Peter showed his badge and asked to see Dominic Rossetti. She excused herself and after a few minutes, returned to escort them upstairs. The elegant stone staircase accentuated the dark hardwood floors. The Rossettis had great taste.

At the top of the stairs, the hostess led them around the corner, and onto thick carpet leading toward offices and a conference room. She stopped at an open door and knocked on the jamb. Behind the desk, a large window overlooked the parking lot, and the city beyond.

Dominic Rossetti smiled and stood to greet them, extending his hand.

Peter took it in a quick clasp and introduced himself and Greg. They sank into leather chairs in front of Dominic's massive wooden desk.

"Mr. Rossetti, you have a beautiful location here. If I had your view, I would never get anything done."

Rossetti laughed. "That's why I have my back to it. Now what can I do for you?"

Peter held out Cindy's picture. "Mr. Rossetti, do you know this woman?"

Dominic cradled it in his hand and paused. Was he studying the picture because he wasn't sure if he knew her, or was he trying to decide what to say?

"I don't know her, although she looks familiar. Is

she the woman on TV?"

Of course, he would have seen her on the news. "Yes. Her name was Cindy Carroll. Had you seen her before the news story came out?"

His gaze shifted to the picture again. "I don't think so. Why?"

"Mr. Rossetti, where were you on the night of April twenty-third?"

"Let's see what was on my calendar." He handed back the picture, swiveled to his computer, and hit a few keys. "Oh, yes, the night of the fundraiser. We were at the Sky Lake Hotel."

"We have reason to believe she might have been at the dinner," Peter continued. "Did you see her there? Was she with anyone?"

"I already told you I hadn't seen her before." Dominic's face flushed, and his voice took on an edge. "If she was there, I didn't notice her."

Greg glanced over and wrote a note on his pad, and Peter let the silence grow. "When did you get home?"

Rossetti's fingers drummed on the edge of his desk. "Fairly late, maybe around midnight."

"Can anyone verify this?"

The fingers stilled. "Not that she should have to, but my wife, Maria, was with me. She can verify it. Why are you asking me all these questions?"

Peter leaned back in his chair. Time to reduce the tension. "It's routine, Mr. Rossetti. We're trying to establish the timing of things. Where she was and who she might have been with."

"Oh." Dominic's shoulders relaxed. "Well, I'm sorry I can't be of more help."

"You've been quite helpful. I need to question

someone else..." He turned to Greg who made the pretense of flipping back a couple of pages in his notepad.

"Mr. Carlo Litzi."

Peter turned to Dominic. "I understand he works here. Is he available?"

"Of course. Come with me." He led them down the hall to an office with the same spectacular view. Dominic ushered them in without announcing them first. Perhaps they had seen them in the parking lot.

"Carlo, there are some detectives here to see you. Detectives, this is Carlo Litzi."

Carlo stood and offered his hand. His gaze was still on Dominic though, when he said, "Thank you, Dominic, for bringing them in so promptly."

The sarcasm was not lost on Peter, but Dominic ignored it and left. Peter introduced himself and Greg and then asked the same questions he'd asked Dominic. The answers came easily and swiftly as if he didn't have to think about it, but a natural arrogance—part of his base personality—tinged his words. Man, it would be fun to wipe the smirk off his face.

"Mr. Litzi, we believe Ms. Carroll was trailing some dealers who supplied the drugs that killed her brother. What do you know about that?"

Carlo moved the stapler from the side of his desk to the middle. "Why would I know anything about some little kid who got into something he shouldn't have?" He looked up. "Did you guys investigate this woman? Maybe her brother got into her stash, and she didn't want to admit it? You know how kids like to imitate their older siblings. She may have gotten what she deserved."

Peter hesitated while Greg wrote in his notebook.

"I don't remember mentioning her brother was younger. Mr. Litzi, do you know the Carrolls?"

"Pinon Creek isn't big, Detective. These things get around. I didn't know them personally, but everyone knew when the kid died."

The time for subtlety was over. "Mr. Litzi, did you kill Cindy Carroll?"

Carlo held his gaze. "I didn't even know the woman. She didn't run in my circles, so why would I kill her?"

17

The hospital stayed busy all day. People kept stopping in—the pastor, their friends, and people from the church, even a couple of the kids from the youth group. Their care touched Robin. Of course, none of them knew about the money. Would they come if they did?

Mark's work friends came in again, one or two at a time. No one looked guilty or as though they wished he wouldn't wake up. But how did someone like that look? She needed to know more about them. As much as she thought she knew, she didn't know them well enough to discuss their personal finances. How could she find out more without tipping them off? Maybe Peter could give her some information.

That evening, she cornered him.

"What kinds of questions?" He arched a skeptical brow.

She cleared her throat. "I'm trying to find out what Mark discovered. If he figured out who the leak was, maybe that person set him up."

"I'm working under the same assumption, but why wouldn't he have told me? We've been working on it for months."

"I don't know." She picked up her journal and wrote Mark's coworkers' names, one to a page. "Maybe he didn't have a chance. I know you guys covered the money angle, but could you go over it with me?" When his face closed and he glanced away from her, she jumped in, "In general, no specifics. Let's see…Tammi, Bill, Greg, David, and you and Mark, right? Oh, and of course, Chief Donovan. What about Beth? Did she know?"

Peter met her eyes. "Yeah. Anything the chief knows, Beth knows."

"OK. I know some of them fairly well." Robin flipped to the beginning. Tammi's page. "Tammi must be struggling. She talks about how her husband ran up the bills before she kicked him out. It can't be easy as a single mom without child support. She doesn't appear to have extra money, but if she was paying bills with it, you might not notice." She jotted some notes and glanced up.

His gaze was still on her. "We checked Tammi's credit, and she has a lot of debt. She works another job to pay off some bills, and she's making progress." He stroked his jaw. "But I guess she may have gotten tired of trying and decided to go the easy route."

"So she is a possibility." Robin wrote a few notes and flipped the page. "Bill lives in a nice house but not ritzy, doesn't spend a lot of money on flashy cars or boats or expensive toys." She tapped the page with her pen while she pictured Bill and his wife. "He and Daisy have four kids, and she's a court stenographer. I don't think she works full time. I believe they fight a lot about money though. She told me Bill thinks she has a shopping addiction. She didn't call it that; she called it a problem. And when I was at their house, I noticed every kitchen gadget known to man, or rather woman—which of course, isn't a crime. What do you think about him?"

Peter resettled and crossed his arms. "Bill also has a lot of debt. There hasn't been big payments though, only more debt. I'd say he's struggling to keep his head above water."

She wrote 'lots of debt' and a question mark. "Let's move on. I don't know much about Greg or David. What do you know about them?"

"David's single, lives in a trendy apartment, and drives an SUV. He has nice clothes and some fun toys, but nothing someone with no one else to support couldn't handle. He doesn't flash money around."

Robin wrote 'single, no influx of money', and turned the page.

"As for Greg, he has money. We checked it out before." Peter ran a hand over his face. "His parents died and left him a few acres in Montana. He sold it to some celebrity for a bundle and invested. He works more for something to do than because he needs the money. I can't imagine him taking such a risk."

"What about Beth and the chief? Beth wears expensive clothes and drives a sports car. Where does she live?"

"Pinon Heights."

Robin raised her brows. "That's the most expensive part of the city! Where does she get the money? I doubt the department pays her much. Going by what they pay my husband at least."

Peter yawned.

She couldn't blame him. He'd been over all this before. If there was something obvious, he and Mark would have found it. "The money and the house belong to her aunt. Do you remember her?" When she nodded, he went on. "Janice lives in Sunny View Retirement Home. She lets Beth live in her house rent-free. Since Beth is her heir, Janice figured Beth might as well start taking care of her inheritance. She also gave her the money for the car." He lowered his arms and slapped a rhythm on his thighs. "Beth doesn't have to spend the money she earns on anyone but herself. We checked her accounts, and she has quite a bit of money. The amount for the car was deposited in Beth's account, and a corresponding sum removed from Janice's. We asked Janice, and she verified she gave Beth the car as a gift."

"That takes care of Beth. What about the chief? He has plenty of money." Robin voiced that thought before Peter changed his mind and clammed up.

Peter remained silent. Had she pushed too far? Seconds passed before he exhaled. "He does, but he makes quite a bit more than we do, too. We were trying to subtly check on him, but it's pretty hard. We did the best we could without being obnoxious. He even wanted us to. I don't think it's him, Robin." He shifted, seeming uncomfortable with more than his seat. "He's the one who looks like a fool having a traitor in the department and not being able to find him. He gave us his account numbers and even called the bank and told them to cooperate. He made up some story for them about an audit or something. No, I'm sure it's not him. He wants this person caught more than anyone."

She snapped her journal closed. She shouldn't feel let down. After all, if it had been easy, Mark would have solved it already. "Well, that takes care of everyone except you and Mark, and I know neither one of us has any extra money." She started to laugh and then stopped, remembering the briefcase in the closet. She cleared her throat. "So, where does this get us?

Money had to play a part—why else would anyone take such a risk?"

"That was our theory, too, but someone covered their tracks pretty well. Who knows what accounts they may have in another name?"

"Did you guys have a theory? Were you close to catching someone?"

"No, that's the strange part. We still don't have a clue who the leak is or who they're covering for, so why would they set up Mark? I know he didn't tell you where he was going, but was there anything earlier?"

She thought back, trying to remember the days before the shooting. Nothing came. "I've been wracking my brain, but I can't think of a thing he said to make sense of this. I came home late the night before, and we didn't have much time to talk. I think he would've said something if he'd had a major breakthrough."

Peter pushed to his feet. "Well, now you know as much as I do, which isn't much. Let me know if you come up with any ideas. I'm open to suggestions." He gave a slight wave and trudged out the door.

She needed to go home and get dinner. Heart heavy, she left the hospital. The doctors said Mark could still wake up and be fine, but the longer he lay there oblivious, the scarier it grew. As she crossed the parking lot, Chief Donovan stepped from his car and headed toward the entrance. She sighed when he didn't see her. She was too tired to catch up, and if she did, she didn't know what else there was to say.

At home, she dropped her keys and purse on the table by the stairs and looked up, remembering a light being on in her closet the other night. She didn't remember turning it on. Sometimes she forgot to turn it off in the winter when she had to leave in the dark, but mornings were getting lighter earlier now, and she hadn't needed it.

Her heart beat faster. Did it mean someone had been in the house? Had they left the light on when they planted the briefcase? *Robin, this is getting farfetched.* Mark must have put it there for a reason, and she must have turned the light on without remembering it. There wasn't a logical alternative.

Silvia called from the kitchen. "Robin, is that you, honey? I have dinner on the stove. It should be ready in a minute."

Heavenly smells wafted from the kitchen. She suppressed a sigh. Now she understood why men didn't want their wives to work. Well, some men anyway. Walking into a house that smelled like home cooking, and sitting down to a meal without having to lift a finger was heaven, plain and simple. And she was so tired.

She doubted she could carry on a coherent conversation, but they talked a lot about Mark. Both Silvia and Ed were positive he'd wake up. They had prayed, and they said they had peace about it.

If only she possessed some of their peace right now. Even if he was OK, the Internal Affairs thing…How would they deal with it? Of course, if he woke up, he'd explain everything. When…*when* he woke up, not *if* he woke up.

Still, the money subject nagged. She shouldn't bring it up, but it continued nagging until Silvia brought homemade apple pie and set it before her.

"Do you guys think someone could have planted the money?" Robin asked.

"Yes." Silvia's face creased into a smile as she fell

into the seat across from Robin. "I couldn't figure out why no one mentioned it earlier."

Ed smiled at his wife, patted her hand, and then faced Robin. "Do you have a theory?"

"Nothing concrete, but I don't remember turning my closet light on that morning. I know it's crazy. But Mark has a thing about me remembering to turn it off, and I've developed the habit of not using it unless I have to. It's been light outside when I've dressed the last couple of weeks, so I haven't had to use it." She stabbed a piece of apple. "But that's ridiculous. I must have. Someone couldn't get in here and plant it without anyone noticing."

"Maybe someone did notice, but no one's asked them. Have you talked to your neighbors?"

Robin's stopped, the fork midway to her mouth. "No, I never considered it. Do you think the police checked with them?"

"Maybe not about that. They've probably asked some questions, but I doubt they asked about that."

"I'll check with them tomorrow. Maybe someone saw something." Relieved they didn't laugh at her or think she was overreacting, she braved bringing up the rest of her fears. Her father-in-law was in midsentence when she blurted, "What about after?"

Ed had picked up his plate and was walking to the sink. He paused and turned. "After what?"

"After Mark wakes up. What'll happen then? We've been focused on getting him to wake up, but what if when he does, they try to pin the murder on him?" She paused. "I'm scared."

"We've been worried about the same thing." Ed set his plate on the counter and came back for hers. "Ever since they searched the house, I haven't felt the same about Mark's friends. I think he's safe for the moment since the guard camped outside his door isn't from his unit. I feel a little better for now."

"You're right. It has to be someone in the group." Robin placed her plate into his outstretched hand. "I don't want to believe it though. We've all grown so close. I can't imagine any of them doing it."

"What do we know about these people?" Ed asked.

They listed the names and what they knew, which wasn't a lot.

Robin had spent some time with the women at barbecues and social events she and Mark participated in. Though she didn't know them well, she told her in-laws what she knew.

Silvia jumped up. "Ed, do you remember when Joe sent Greg out to live with a relative or something? Rumor was drugs were involved."

"Yeah, I do remember something. Robin, did Mark ever say anything about it?" She must have looked confused. Ed didn't wait for her response. "It was just before we moved to Wyoming. Greg and some other kids got caught doing drugs or something. It was all hushed up, and Joe sent him off to Montana or someplace 'til things calmed down. I wonder if it went on his record or if the police chief knows about it."

With that thought, Robin went upstairs, washed her face, and pulled some clean clothes out to take back to the hospital with her. She pictured Cindy—young, pretty, in her early twenties. Detective Thompson suggested Mark thought Cindy was more attractive than her. Did he enjoy flirting with her?

She jerked back a step. She knew Mark better than that, didn't she? He wasn't the flirty type. And from what she'd heard so far, neither was Cindy, especially not with married men.

What about Greg? Did he know Cindy? Could they have been working together? Maggie was beginning to like him. She hoped he wouldn't disappoint her. She headed back to the hospital and her familiar cot. Sleep didn't come easy, and at 2:00 AM, Mark woke up.

18

Robin, sleeping on the cot next to Mark's bed, heard him stir and sat up. His breathing increased and the monitor beeped. She leapt to her feet and stood over him, her hand to her mouth, her heart beating in her chest. She wanted to grab his hand, but she was afraid to touch him.

A nurse hurried in, observed him for a moment and shut off the machine.

His eyelids fluttered, then opened. It took a couple minutes before he focused on her face.

The nurse moved closer to check.

Robin stepped back to give her some room, and sniffled, trying to stop the tears streaming down her face.

He reached up to finger the feeding tube, but the nurse stopped him from pulling it out. She wrote something on his chart, and said the doctor would be in right away.

Mark smiled and reached for Robin. She half lay on the bed, trying not to dislodge the apparatus that had fed him for the last four days. "You scared me to death! I thought I was going to lose you, and I didn't think I could bear it. Don't ever do that to me again!"

He smoothed her hair, and she kissed his hands, wanting so badly to hold him. Instead she sobbed. He stroked her back. When she got control of herself, she stood and smiled at him.

The doctor came in.

Robin slipped out to make her calls. There'd be no more sleep tonight. When Robin returned to Mark's cube, the feeding tube was gone, but his throat was raw, and he had trouble speaking without coughing. She tried to avoid the questions in his eyes while helping him sip some water.

Finally, he got out a raspy whisper. "What happened?" he croaked. "Car accident?"

Robin's face froze. How did you tell someone they'd been shot? Thankfully, her in-laws, and Peter and Maggie showed up. Everyone took turns being with Mark when he was awake and keeping her company while he slept.

He drifted in and out the rest of the night, falling asleep sometimes in the middle of someone's sentence.

Silvia's reaction was similar to Robin's—she couldn't stop crying. Respect for her mother-in-law grew as Robin realized how hard it must have been for her to step back these last few days and let Robin stay at Mark's bedside.

Maggie left around six to get the group breakfast, and while they were eating, Mark woke up hungry. He didn't get to eat what they were eating, and he didn't eat much. But he ate a little, and that bit of normalcy was a gift. A gift from God.

The doctor came in just before lunch. While Mark's throat was still sore, he could communicate somewhat better. "So, Mark, we're all happy to see you with your eyes open. How do you feel?"

"My head is killing me...shoulder feels like hit...sledgehammer. Otherwise, OK."

The doctor sat next to his bed and wrote on a

clipboard. "What is the last thing you remember?"

Mark raised his gaze to the ceiling. "Went to bed last night...woke up here. Robin says...shot...don't remember."

The doctor explained when he'd been admitted, and Mark's face scrunched. He put his hand to his head as if the information hurt. "Four days?"

A pang hit Robin. How would she tell him he was under investigation for murder? Could such a shock cause a relapse or something? He watched her while he was awake, which wasn't often. His friends would probably stop in later, and she needed to tell him before one of them did. She was exhausted, and her head pounded. Confiding her fears to her mother-in-law, she left Silvia to stand guard over him and went home to take a nap.

19

Peter left for work, straight from the hospital. Having been up since 3:00 AM, and not getting tons of sleep the previous nights, his body began to show it. He felt sluggish. If he sat down, he'd go right to sleep. He headed for the coffee machine. He wanted to people watch at the 9:00 AM progress meeting. Sipping his coffee, he slipped into the conference room and hovered. He could see the desks, and hear what was said, without being too noticeable.

Even an hour early, he hadn't beat Tammi. She hunched over her desk doing paperwork.

Bill wandered in, rubbing his eyes and stopped by her desk. "How long you been here?" he asked.

"Couple hours." She glanced up, eyes bright.

His desk sat in front of hers, so he swiveled his chair and faced her. "Didn't you say you were working security last night?"

"Yeah. But they let some of us go early, so I got home around midnight."

Peter grunted. She got home at midnight and still managed to get to work by six? No wonder she had circles under her eyes.

"So what was going on at the event center last night?"

"Nothing special. Some Denver group rented it out for their conference. Lots of people, but nothing controversial. So, like I said, they cut us loose early. I was kinda hopin' for a couple more hours—the money's good, and you don't have to do anything but walk around. It's a great gig."

Bill smiled and turned away.

Tammi continued to work.

Peter left the security of the conference room and wandered around. Maybe whoever brought donuts for the meeting set them out early. He headed for the squad room, only to hang back when he saw that Bill had the same idea.

David was already in there laying napkins next to open doughnut boxes.

"So, your turn for breakfast, huh?" Bill said, pouring himself some coffee.

"Yeah, and they smelled so good in the car I just about ate one. Help yourself, so I can say I waited."

"I'm happy to oblige." Bill picked up a donut and bit into it.

Peter's stomach growled.

"Have you heard anything about Mark yet?" David crammed a whole donut into his mouth.

"No, but I plan to go by today. Do you want to tag along?"

David chewed for a minute then opened his mouth without swallowing. "When are you going, after work?"

Bill glanced away, and Peter chuckled to himself. He'd had the same experience. David was good to have around if one was on a diet.

"Probably around lunch," Bill said.

"Never mind then. I'm going after my shift. I want to talk to Peter, and he's usually there about then."

Bill jerked his head toward the conference room

Peter had just left. "I don't think you'll have to go to the hospital to see Peter. He's here somewhere."

So much for remaining unseen.

David lowered his voice, and Peter strained to hear. "Hey, did you hear they searched his house? They found all kinds of money in a briefcase."

"You mean Mark's?" Bill took another bite. "Yeah, I heard."

"So what do you think? Was it Mark or are you like some who think it was all a setup?"

Bill dusted some crumbs off the front of his shirt. "I don't know what you mean about a setup, but I know one of the officers who found the money. And there were witnesses. They couldn't all have been in on it."

David leaned in. Peter caught a few words. "I...searchers, but...somebody. A lot of people...Mark...involved."

"What do you think?" Bill stepped back.

"I never trust anyone who's that good, you know?" David shoved another doughnut in his mouth and proceeded to talk around it. "Nobody's that perfect. And money corrupts people. Look at all those television evangelists. Greed, that's all it is. Preachers trying to tell you how to live, when they can't even manage to keep themselves straight."

"I wondered about that. Mark's into religion big time." He took a sip from his cup. "So do you think Mark is like that? Do you think he did it?" He moved toward the tables set up classroom style with all the chairs facing the front. "Let's find a table."

David followed.

Peter slunk back a little farther.

"I don't know if Mark did it or not," David said,

"but I'm not counting anybody out, not even your partner."

"Tammi?" Bill stopped in the middle of an aisle. "What makes you think it's her?"

David nearly bumped into Bill, sloshing coffee out onto the floor. "I didn't say I thought it was her, but I overheard her talking to herself and she said something like 'it will all be worth it.' I don't think she realized she'd said it, let alone loud enough for someone to hear." He moved around Bill. "I know she's your partner and all, but how good can a woman be at a job like this? No wonder she's having trouble. Maybe she's letting someone in on what she knows so she can go home and do what she's good at."

Bill backed away, looking around to see if they had been overheard. "I can't believe you said that. Tammi is awesome at her job, and she works another one besides. She works harder than all of us put together, and I don't think she could betray her unit, even if you do." Bill turned away from David.

"Hey, I didn't mean anything. You don't have to get mad," David called after him.

Peter slipped out the back, as other people were filing in. Did David honestly suspect Tammi? If so, it wouldn't be a stretch to suspect Bill. Wonder if Bill knew that? And what would he do about it?

Chief Donovan entered the room and walked to the podium. Tammi trailed behind him, and chose a seat near the front. Peter hurried outside, walked around to the front, entered, and stood in an alcove behind Donovan where he could see everyone's faces.

Donovan hesitated, waiting for the ones who were standing around talking to find their seats. "I have good news this morning. Mark's awake and doing well. The doctor thinks he'll be fine."

Claps, whistles, and general commotion erupted for several minutes.

Then David asked the obvious question. "So are we going to make an arrest now or what?"

He couldn't see Donovan's face, but everyone else was smiling.

"Not yet. I talked to Robin and the doctor, and Mark's not ready to answer questions yet. Apparently, he's awake for short periods at a time, but it's hard for him to talk, and it appears he doesn't remember what happened to him."

Everyone started talking at once.

Peter couldn't make out anything.

Donovan shuffled through his papers and withdrew one. He cleared his throat, and the room quieted, everyone attentive and eager.

Peter studied his coworkers' faces, searching for the telltale sign someone wasn't pleased Mark was awake. Out there, looking back at the chief, was the face of Judas. But nothing gave him or her away, not a frown, not a facial tic, nothing. Everyone appeared happy, elated even. Whoever the leak was must be a good actor...very, very good.

"The doctor said it wasn't unusual for someone who has undergone head trauma to suffer temporary amnesia," Donovan said. "Let's see how he does, and when we know something concrete, we'll take action. I don't want Mark's condition spread around yet. I know it'll get out, but I'd like to keep it from the general public as long as possible." He then started on the week's assignments.

Peter left the room.

20

While Donovan finished up, Peter slipped into the chief's office to wait.

It didn't take long. Donovan blew in and closed the door. "I'm glad you're here," he said putting his notes down on the desk. "Tell me. Where are we with the investigation?"

Peter told him about the interviews with Cindy's mom and friend.

"So you think she wasn't actually at the dinner?" Donovan settled in his chair.

"We've questioned many of the guests, and no one saw her there. Plus, her clothes suggest she wasn't a guest, unless she changed first. Based on what I heard from her best friend, I think she followed someone, waited until they came out, and then trailed them to the warehouse."

"Did they say who she might have been following?"

"No, but Dominic Rossetti was there that night."

Donovan sat up straighter. "That's interesting. Have you questioned him yet?"

"Yeah, but we can't prove a link existed between them. Same with his smug business manager, Carlo Litzi. I'd sure love to knock the cocky smile off his face. He's dirty, and he knows I know it. But he also knows I can't prove it." Peter tapped the arm of his chair. "We might be able to lean on Rossetti. He was nervous, I can tell you that much."

Donovan peered into Peter's eyes. "Keep me informed. Internal Affairs and the mayor are breathing down my neck. We have to find something soon. Since Mark's awake, they'll want to move on an arrest warrant."

Peter jerked in his chair. "A warrant? They want to arrest Mark, the guy with the perfect record. The guy they loved for taking down the pusher in the same ring we're looking for now. Does the mayor know how ridiculous this is?"

"Internal Affairs feels they have a solid case with the cash and the unlicensed gun. Unless Mark can explain it, there's nothing I can do. In all probability, they won't tell me when they arrest him." Bitterness tinged every word. "They might be kind enough to inform me after the fact."

Five minutes later, Peter slammed out of the station and accelerated out of the parking lot. How could the department believe Mark would arrest one dealer but save the others? It didn't make sense. It was a quick solution, and they didn't care if it was wrong.

He drummed his fingers on the steering wheel. How could he keep them from arresting Mark? Even if they eventually found him innocent, people would think he did it and the department covered it up. And later he would remember that the people he'd worked so hard to serve had turned on him. It couldn't happen. Peter couldn't allow it to happen. He had to do something, but what? What was he missing?

21

The alarm clock by Robin's bed said three o'clock, later than she'd planned. She glanced at Mark's empty place beside her and touched his pillow. He'd finally awakened—or had it been a dream? She swung her legs over the side of the bed, grabbed her clothes, and scrambled into them.

Minutes later, at the hospital, she all but ran to Mark's room.

He waggled his fingers at her as she entered, dispelling her fears.

Her whole body sagged as she shuffled closer. "Hi," she whispered and settled in the chair beside his bed. She glanced at him, ready to fend off his questions, but he was asleep.

Tammi and Bill stopped by a few minutes later. They hovered in the doorway with a huge bouquet of flowers. Not wanting to wake him, Robin met them in the hall. She waited as the officer wrote down their names and the time. "So," she said, "did you guys hear the news?"

Tammi handed over the flowers. "Yeah, we heard he's awake. Does it mean he'll be OK?"

"He's doing great." Robin's smile felt as if it took up her whole face. She took the flowers and danced them into Mark's room, remembering to be quiet as she placed them carefully on the windowsill. She tiptoed back out. "He still falls asleep a lot, sometimes in the middle of a sentence, but the doctor thinks he'll be fine." She glanced at the police officer and jerked her head toward the waiting room. "Let's talk in there so we don't wake him up. It's funny, you know? We tried so hard to wake him up before, and now I want him to sleep."

Tammi fell in step beside her. "Yeah, circumstances have sure changed. I hear he doesn't remember anything. Is that right? Nothing?"

Robin glanced back at Bill to include him in the conversation. "That's right. He remembers going to bed the night before and then nothing until he woke up here."

They reached the waiting room.

"Wow," Bill said. "That is really weird. Does the doctor think he'll get his memory back?"

Robin found a seat, and they sat next to her. She didn't know what to say. If Mark continued to have amnesia, would that keep him safe? "I don't know. The doctor said it's hard to predict at this point."

Tammi smiled. "I'm sure he will. He's such a great guy. The department isn't the same without him."

"Yeah." Bill nodded. "We all miss him. And we'll get whoever did this to him."

Robin leaned in close. "I'm relieved to hear you say so."

Bill leaned back, eyes widening. "What do you mean?"

She picked a piece of lint off her jeans. "You know Internal Affairs thinks he got himself shot trying to sell drugs."

Both of them remained quiet for a second.

Tammi shook her head. "We had heard that, but

it's crazy. It makes me mad they're so ready to believe the worst."

Bill put his hand on Robin's arm. "It's IA's job to focus on one of us, but that doesn't mean the rest of the department isn't still looking outside for the killer."

Robin wanted to ask them what they thought about the money, but she didn't have the nerve. What would she say if they told her they thought he was guilty? They made small talk and then left, leaving her wondering. If what Tammi said was true, not everyone believed Mark was a killer. But Bill's answer was strange. Did they think Mark was hiding something? And was there another meaning behind Tammi's "circumstances have changed" remark?

David came in later, this time with a plant. Robin accepted it, and since Mark was awake, allowed him to come in and visit. She didn't want to bring up the case for fear of upsetting Mark, so she didn't get a chance to talk to David. He didn't act as if he believed Mark was guilty, but she couldn't tell. He did ask her if she'd seen Beth yet.

"No why? Is she coming in?"

"Her aunt fell last night at the nursing home and broke a hip. They were supposed to operate on her today."

"Oh, no! The few times we've met, I liked her. I hope she'll be OK." She'd have to visit Janice as soon as they put her in a room. It might cheer her up, and it would do Robin good to stop worrying about her own problems for a while.

Beth came in around four thirty and said her aunt was stable and in intensive care for observation. Mark was asleep, so she didn't stay. She said she hoped Mark was feeling better and left.

Robin realized how bad the case against Mark was becoming when Maggie came in and she had a chance to talk it through. Mark had been out more than he'd been awake today, and she didn't want to discuss the case with a policeman right outside the door. So she led Maggie to the waiting room.

Maggie barely waited for her to sit before asking, "What'd you learn?"

"What?"

"The funeral. Did you learn anything?"

She seemed so hopeful, Robin almost hated to let her down. "Not really. The turnout was huge. She must have been well liked."

Maggie's expression fell slightly, then became carefully neutral. She sat in the chair next to Robin.

"There was one thing. Cindy's mom said little Joey had wanted to talk to the chief, but he died before he got a chance."

Maggie leaned toward her. "What do you think that was all about?"

"I don't know."

"Did she say what he wanted to tell him?"

"No, but she didn't act worried about it."

Maggie pleated the bottom of her shirt between her fingers. "Do you know if Mark visited him that day?"

Robin frowned. "Everyone knows Joey liked Mark. He's good with kids." Thompson's remarks tried to intrude, but she pushed them away. "I remember how upset he was after Joey died, but I can't remember if he saw him that day or not."

"It's been almost a year now. If Mark learned anything, he would have told you back then." Maggie sprang from her chair and paced. "What if someone did get a chance to talk to Joey, and he shared what he knew with the wrong person? What could a little boy know that would incriminate someone?" She flopped back into her chair. "This is too confusing."

Robin shook her head to clear it. "I hate this. These are Mark's friends. How could one of them be guilty of murder?"

Maggie left with neither of them any closer to the truth. That evening Robin finally got some time alone with Mark. The flow of visitors had stopped, so they shouldn't be disturbed, but she wanted to ensure some privacy. She poked her head into the hall.

"I'm going to close the door. I want to talk to Mark for a bit."

Jack, the officer on duty, nodded, and she eased the door closed.

"Hmm, what's running through that cute little head of yours?" Mark asked with a wicked grin.

"Not that. You're in no condition, and I'm too tired." A glimmer of sunshine pushed back the darkness in her mind and broke free on her face. "Besides, we might make people in the other rooms jealous."

He chuckled, the lighthearted sound she had missed the last few days. "Then tell me, what will we do?"

The moment felt so fragile, she hesitated to break it. She wanted to pretend none of this had happened and just banter, but he wouldn't thank her for waiting. How could she start? "I have something to tell you."

"I gathered that. Is it good?"

She twisted her wedding ring around her finger. "No, it isn't. I haven't let anyone tell you this, but I think you need to know what's been going on." Once she started, she couldn't stop. She began with the money they found in his pockets and kept going. When she told him Internal Affairs questioned her, anger exploded on his face. But he kept quiet until she told him everything.

Almost everything. "Oh, and Isaiah Thompson accused you of having an affair with Cindy Carroll." The tears finally burst forth and ran down her face. He made room for her on the bed, and she climbed in and snuggled up. His arms pulled her in close, and she relaxed against him.

He held her until she stopped crying and then gave her a gentle squeeze. "Honey, you know I'd never have an affair. I love you too much. And with Cindy Carroll? Are they kidding? She's not even out of college." He stroked her arm. "What could Thompson be thinking? He must have been trying to turn you against me so you would tell them something."

She bent forward and peered up at him. "He knew about my divorce and about Carl cheating on me. He must've known it would be a sore spot."

Mark's kiss was tender as he tucked her back under his arm. "I can't believe he put you through that." He carefully rested his head against the pillows. "I can see why he got a search warrant after finding so much money in my pocket. I have no idea where it came from. I know I didn't have it the night before, and from what the doctor said, it was too early for me to have gone to the bank. It had to be planted so they would search the house. So where did the other money come from? And how did they get it in your closet? Maybe we can find something from the briefcase. If IA will let us. Sorry, didn't mean to think out loud." He gave her another quick squeeze. "I know it's impossible, but try not to worry. Peter and I will figure it out."

She relaxed. The worry would come back of course, but for now, she let it go. Snuggling in closer, she changed the subject.

He followed her lead and talked about other things, but his mind seemed elsewhere.

A tap on the door signaled the end of their quiet time, and Ed poked his head in. "Do you want us to come back later?"

"No, of course not. Come in," Robin said.

When Ed opened the door wide, Silvia scooted around him. "OK you two, what are you up to?" Silvia grinned.

"I told him all of it, and this is how he reacted." Robin climbed off the bed, ignoring Mark's hands that didn't want to let go. She smoothed the bedcovers before sitting in the chair. Conversation flowed around her, but she wasn't listening. For a little while, she let the thoughts and fears of the last few days fade. Everything felt right. Still one little question wouldn't go. How long could it last?

22

Robin drove home and, for the first time in days, spent the night in her own bed. She woke early, refreshed and ready to take on the day. A plan had come to her during the night, and she knew the perfect person to help her carry it out.

Maggie answered the phone on the first ring. "What's the matter?"

Robin realized getting a call from her at 7:00 AM must have scared her. "Sorry, nothing's wrong, but I need a favor."

"Anything."

That's why Robin loved her. She told her what she was thinking, and though she could hear the doubt in her voice, Maggie agreed.

"Let me get dressed and I'll pick you up," she said, and good to her word, she arrived thirty minutes later in the Sunshine Interiors van.

"Are you sure this is a good idea? What if we get caught?" Maggie asked.

"I guess we'll figure that out when the time comes. Libby's getting Peter to check out little Joey, so maybe we can check out the police officers in Mark's unit. We're decorators, we're used to sizing people up by the way they keep their house. We can't go inside, but maybe if we drive by we'll get a feel for them on a more personal level."

Maggie shook her head. "If you say so. Where should we go first?"

Robin took out her Christmas card list. "Let's start with Tammi James."

She gave her the address, and Maggie keyed it into her GPS. It didn't take long to get there. The neighborhood was new, with construction still in progress a few blocks away. Though the house was small, it was nice. Maggie drifted to a stop across from the address and put the van in park, allowing it to idle while they took in the cute little two-story. The siding was light gray, with white trim and shutters.

Dare they get out and peek in a window? Robin had just unhooked her seatbelt, when a moving van backed into Tammi's driveway.

"Is this the right address?" Maggie rechecked the GPS.

"Yep, it's the one on my list. Is Tammi moving? Could her finances have deteriorated so bad she had to sell her place?" She felt a tinge of pity at the thought.

A middle-aged woman propped the door open while two men exited the truck. The driver spoke to her while the other man opened the rear and set the ramp. Someone was moving in, not out. The woman strode to the truck. She was tall and slim, an older version of Tammi.

"It must be her mother," Robin said.

Maggie steered away from the curb and drove to the end of the block.

Robin craned her neck to look back. "That's how she's making it without her husband. If her mom moves in, she can get help with the house payment and free daycare. It'll be hard on her though. I don't think they get along all that great."

Maggie dipped her head to enter in the next address. "Maybe her mom moving in is a way to cover extra money."

Robin felt sadness as she drew a line through Tammi's name. "I don't think so." She remembered what Tammi had said at their last barbeque. She could never measure up to her mother's expectations. Living with her must be excruciating. "It would allow her some flexibility, but I don't think it would be enough by itself. I think we can drop her off our list."

Bill's house was in an older part of Pinon Creek, but it was bigger than Tammi's. It needed a paint job, and a twenty-year-old van sat in the driveway. An assortment of bicycles, skateboards, and sports equipment littered the yard.

Maggie parked down the street, and she and Robin got out of the van and jogged back. Robin just had to see inside. Slim, curtain-less windows flanked the door in invitation. Clutching some fliers and business cards, they walked up and Robin peered in, rehearsing what she would say if she got caught.

The living room and dining room looked similar to the outside—full of furniture and toys, crowding a too-small space.

Maggie pretended to put something on the door in case someone was watching, and they calmly but quickly fled past the clutter, to the van.

"So much stuff!" Robin said, waiting for Maggie to hit the door unlock. "A lot to afford on one full-time and one part-time salary."

Maggie climbed in and started the van. "At first, I thought some of it might be from the neighbor kids, but the inside is worse than the outside, and some of it looks pretty expensive. Of course, if the house is paid for that would make a difference."

Robin nodded. "I think you're right. I've been in their house, and it's stuffed with a lot of designer brands. They wear designer labels, too. Let me see my notes." She routed through her bag and lifted out her journal. "Peter says when they did a financial check on Bill they discounted him because his charge cards are all maxed out. That's how he's affording all those designer things."

Maggie made a U-turn out of the neighborhood. "Maybe we shouldn't be writing him off so fast. Mounting bills could be making him desperate. He might have convinced himself he wasn't hurting anyone. Giving information isn't the same as killing someone."

"It is in the eyes of the law if it leads to murder," Robin said. "And he must know that."

"Yeah, but it doesn't take the same cold-bloodedness pulling the trigger and watching someone die would take."

"True." Robin scribbled a note in her journal.

David lived in a second-floor apartment. Two large windows fronted his apartment's white exterior, and he'd left the blinds open. Robin raised to her toes and shaded her eyes to peer inside. The living room and kitchen furniture could have been bought by Bachelor's Are Us—leather, leather, everywhere. A few dishes resided by the coffeemaker. Otherwise, the place was tidy.

Maggie took her turn to peer inside, not having to get on tiptoe do it. "Not much to see here. A single guy's man-cave. Some nice leather though. Looked like pretty good quality, but hard to tell from here."

"I agree. Good quality, but nothing extravagant.

He's not living above his means though, judging by his furnishings." She put a question next to his name and gave Maggie a grin. "Now for the one you want to see."

Greg's apartment was on the top floor of his building in a nice part of town. They rode the elevator up, Robin picturing what his place would look like and drawing a blank.

"What do you think we'll find?" She elbowed her friend in the ribs. "Will electronics have taken over? Is he a neat freak or a slob?"

Maggie huffed and moved away. "I don't know. Let's just get on with it."

The elevator doors opened to a small hallway and a door with the only opening being a peephole. "We're not going to figure him out today," Robin said. "His apartment must take up the entire top floor."

Maggie darted back into the elevator and pushed the down button.

Robin assumed more than anywhere else, Maggie did not want to be caught snooping here. She moved a little slower.

Maggie reached out and dragged her inside. "Would you hurry up?"

Robin laughed.

Back in the vehicle, they drove to Pinon Heights where Chief Donovan and Beth both lived. An exclusive gated community—complete with a guard on duty. Robin glared at the guardhouse as they drove by, her plan of sneaking in on foot evaporating. She didn't need to see their houses. The aura alone was intimidating.

"We should target this neighborhood for the business," she said.

Maggie nodded. "Roger that, partner."

She turned the van toward the hospital. "Apparently, the people with money are Greg, Beth, and Chief Donovan. The chief I can kind of understand. After all, he probably makes quite a bit, and he's single. But Beth I don't understand and, I hate to say it, Greg. Beth lives in the Heights, for heaven's sake. How on earth does she afford it?" She scowled at Robin. "And Greg lives in the penthouse of a pricey building."

Robin flipped through her notes. "According to Peter, Beth lives in her aunt's house and takes care of it for her. Janice lives in a nursing home, and the trust handles all the bills. Beth can spend what she makes on herself."

Maggie bit her lip as she turned into the hospital lot and found a parking place. "That leaves Greg." The lightness in her voice seemed forced. "Wouldn't you know it? I'm attracted to a possible drug dealer."

Robin laughed. "Don't get too worked up yet. Greg received an inheritance from his uncle."

Hope flared in Maggie's eyes and then died. "That's a little convenient, isn't it? I hate to say so, but he makes the most sense."

Robin watched her face. It felt like she was delivering a bombshell on her best friend. "Ed told me about a scandal involving Greg as a boy." She lowered her voice. "He was sent away as a teenager, and Ed thinks it involved drugs."

Maggie eyed her nails. "Why do I even care? It's not like I had any kind of relationship with him." Her face took on a faraway look "Although he doesn't seem like a drug dealer. I can't explain it, but he seems kind."

Robin touched Maggie's arm. "We have no proof he's the leak. So far all we have are rumors." She let go and went on quickly. "I think we need to talk to the chief. I wanted to talk to him anyway about Joey and ask him what he's heard from Internal Affairs."

Maggie nodded, her eyes getting a misty look.

Robin snickered, trying to lighten things up a bit. "I desperately want to ask what he's doing to investigate, but I don't know how to go about it." She braced her elbows on her knees. "How do you tell the chief of police you think he's not doing a good enough job—especially when he's your husband's boss?" She unlatched her seatbelt and reached for the door handle. "Thanks for everything. It helps to have someone to talk to who isn't police. I need someone objective to tell me when I'm getting crazy."

Maggie smiled. "You are crazy, but it's nothing new. You've been crazy since I met you."

Robin laughed, and got out of the van.

Maggie left without going back in to see Mark. If Greg was there, she probably didn't want to see him. She pushed her friend's hurting face out of her mind. She hated doing that to her. But if Greg was not what he said he was, she deserved to know now.

23

Peter exhaled. He was on his way to see Virginia Carroll again. How had he let Libby talk him into this? Bringing up this subject would be painful, and it had probably been covered thoroughly at the time. But if checking it out again brought the smallest thing to light, it would be worth it.

He had called first, so she was expecting him, but he didn't get out of the car right away. He checked his notes for exactly what Robin said she'd heard. Joey had wanted to see the chief, but he died before he could.

Virginia answered the door and let him in, extending her hand.

Peter shook it gently and then covered it with his other hand. "I'm so sorry to disturb you again, Virginia. But like I said on the phone, I think it would help give us the whole picture if we knew more about Joey."

Virginia showed him into the living room and sat in the same place on the couch as she had the last time.

He sank into a recliner across from her.

An eight by ten picture of Cindy now graced the table next to the couch. Virginia reached for the picture and stroked the glass with her finger. "I want to get to the bottom of this. If the same person or people are behind the deaths of my children, I want them stopped. What do you want to know?"

Peter checked his notes. "At the funeral, someone said Joey had wanted to see the chief but didn't get a chance before he died. Is that correct?"

She nodded. "He said he had something to tell him. I wasn't crazy about interrupting the chief, but he'd given me his card, so I called after lunch. He said he had an event or something that night, but he'd come by the next day." Her voice was husky, and she cleared her throat. "He'd been doing so well. We had no idea he would go that fast."

"Did anyone come to see Joey the day he died?"

"I don't think so. I told the police officer that at the time. They were hoping to find out what Joey wanted to tell Chief Donovan, but he never told me. As far as I know he didn't tell anyone else either."

Peter leaned forward clasping his hands together, trying to make his posture as nonthreatening as possible. "No one came, not the police, not anyone?"

Her finger stilled, and she glanced up. "His friend Tim came to see him. He was pretty shaken up after Joey died, because he had seemed so strong that morning. We all thought he was getting better. I think Tim took it as hard as Cindy did."

Again, Peter kept his voice gentle. "Did the police question him that you know of?"

"They probably did, but I don't know. I can give you his address if you'd like." She went to the kitchen and returned with an old-fashioned address book.

He wrote the address in his notes. Virginia couldn't remember anything else about that day, so he thanked her and left her standing at the door. A cat rubbed against her leg and she picked it up, gently stroking its fur. Joey's or Cindy's pet? He didn't want to know.

He parked in front of Tim's house, a small two-story. Glancing around at the well-maintained yard, he walked up the flower-bordered path and rang the bell. When a thirtyish woman answered the door, he spoke through the screen, introducing himself and showing her his badge.

"Are you Mrs. Walsh? Tim's mother?"

"Yes. Can you tell me what this is about?"

"As you've probably heard, Cindy Carroll was murdered. It's become known that Joey may have had something to tell the police. I just want to check with Tim to see if Joey told him anything that might be useful."

"I don't think so—if he had, Timmy would have already told them."

"It's a long shot, I agree. I just want to get a sense of what was happening that day and anything he remembers. I have sons of my own. I'll be gentle with him. I promise."

"I guess it's OK. He's in the kitchen getting a snack." She opened the screen door and stepped back to let him in. "Please don't upset him. He was devastated when his friend died, and he still isn't over it. I wouldn't let you bring it all up again if it weren't for Joey's big sister."

He followed her through a spotless, modern living room, the light-colored furniture contrasting with the dark hardwood floors.

She paused at the doorway to the family room and turned to him. "He's already distressed about Cindy. I'll let you start, but if he gets upset, I want you to stop."

After giving his word, Peter entered the room and waited on the couch for her to get her son. This is where they lived. The furniture was a darker, more kid-friendly color, and a large area rug covered a space in front of the TV. Perfect for playing games.

Tim entered behind his mother, and Peter hid a smile. Tim could have been one of Peter's kids, red hair and all. His face was solemn as his mother explained who Peter was and why he wanted to talk to him.

Tim stood in front of him. "You're a policeman?"

Peter nodded.

"Why don't you have a uniform on?"

He tried to keep from laughing. "I'm a detective."

"Like Mark?"

So he did remember him. "Yes, just like Mark. Tim, is it OK if I ask you about Joey?"

Tim nodded, his face serious.

Peter didn't want to spook him or his mother, so he braced his arms on his knees and let his hands dangle. "What can you remember about the last time you went to visit him?"

Tim fidgeted with the bottom of his shirt, stretching the t-shirt material and rolling it over his fists. "Not too much. We played a board game—his favorite."

Peter smiled, wondering at the old-fashioned game. Had they made it into a computer game? "No, I didn't. Is it your favorite as well?"

"It's a pretty cool game, but I like chess right now. I'm learning to play with my brother, but he always beats me."

"Big brothers are like that."

Tim's hands stilled, wrapped in his shirt. "How did you know he was my big brother?"

"Just a guess. So, do you remember what you talked about?"

He unrolled the material. "Not really. The policemen wanted me to tell them, too, but it wasn't nothing important. He didn't tell me what he wanted to talk to the chief about. I didn't even know he wanted to. He must have told his mom, and maybe the blonde lady he used to talk to."

"There was a blonde lady?"

"Yeah. This recess lady who used to help at lunchtime sometimes, and talk to the kids. They liked her a lot. She never talked to me though."

"Is she still at the school? Have you seen her lately?"

"No, she isn't there now."

Peter tried to make his voice light. "Was there anyone else Joey talked to?"

"I don't think so. But I wasn't around him all the time, you know? He might have, and I wouldn't know." Tim started to fidget. He was at the end of his attention span.

"One more quick question. Did Mark ever talk to Joey?"

"Yeah, I remember Mark. He's cool. He talked to all of us. Joey liked him a lot. Hey, do you like baseball?"

"Yes, I do. Who's your favorite?"

"I like the local team."

"A fan, eh? They're my favorite team, too."

They talked a little more about baseball, and then Peter left. Walking to his car, he checked his watch. He might be able to catch Libby before she picked the kids up from soccer practice. He hadn't seen her much since the shooting.

When he got home, she stopped vacuuming and sat at the kitchen table with him. She popped up to get them some iced tea and finally settled across from him.

He gulped half of his glass.

She waited calmly. "Did you find out anything?"

He placed one hand on both of hers. He hated letting her down. "Remember, you promised not to get your hopes up."

Her face fell. "She didn't remember anything? I know we weren't expecting much, but I hoped she'd think of something helpful."

He gave her hands a squeeze and released them. "She gave me the name of a friend who had visited him that day, and I went to see him. You would have loved him. He looked just like Danny did at that age."

Libby sipped her tea. "And…?"

"He didn't remember. But he said something about a blonde lunch lady Joey used to talk to. I scanned the old file before I went, but I don't remember anything about her."

"That's something though, isn't it? Can you check on her?" She wiped her hand on the tablecloth. "She might have been a part-timer or a volunteer."

"I can try. Who knows if they'll have a record if she was a volunteer, but I can check it out. Sure."

She smiled. "I know it's probably nothing. I just feel so helpless.…" She carried the glasses to the sink.

"I know." He stood behind her, folded his arms around her waist, and nuzzled her neck. "Let's call Linda and see if she can pick up the kids. Tell her we can get them later. We can take advantage of some alone time and not talk about the case."

"What a great idea." She turned in his arms. "What do you want to talk about?"

He pulled her close. "I wasn't thinking about talking."

24

Mark flipped through the channels one more time. Nothing on. The sitcom he'd been watching couldn't hold his interest, and he didn't feel like reading. He turned it off and reached for his phone, studying the pictures Peter had sent him of the warehouse. Cindy's body wasn't in them, but her outline and blood stains were there, and the stains by the entrance must be his. Peter didn't send him those at first, but Mark insisted.

A feeling of desolation filled him again as he remembered the sweet young girl so engaged in finding her brother's killers. He could almost see her earnest face the times he'd talked to her before. He scrolled back to the pictures of the warehouse. Why couldn't he remember being there?

He leaned back against the pillows, closing his eyes, trying to remember. He focused on the warehouse, but he could only remember what was in the pictures. The rest was a blank. A big nothing.

Sounds of laughing children being shushed by their parents filtered in from the corridor as a family passed his room. It must be time for visiting hours to end.

He dozed a little then startled awake, unsure what woke him.

Chief Donovan stood at the door, hand raised to knock.

Mark gave him a welcoming smile. "Chief, come in. It's good to see you."

Mark pushed the button to raise the bed.

Donovan put his hand up. "Don't get up. I don't want to disturb you. I can come back tomorrow."

"No, come in. I can use the company."

Donovan's face was full of questions, but when he met Mark's gaze, he stopped himself.

Mark probably looked similar to how he felt—like road kill.

Donovan gave him a slow smile. "So, slugger, when will you be ready to play first base? The team's missing you."

Mark chuckled. "I feel more like I could be first base, actually. The doctor says since I wasn't unconscious too long, the recovery shouldn't be too bad. But I want to know how bad is 'too bad,' and too bad for whom?" He plumped his pillows and lay back. "I'm glad you're here. I want to talk to you while Robin's gone."

"Did she go home?"

"She did, but it took all my powers of persuasion. She looks as bad as I do, although if you tell her I said so, I'll deny it."

Donovan laughed. "She's a pretty special lady, you know." He settled in. "I wouldn't want to cross her where you're concerned. She defends you like a tigress."

And now they'd reached the heart of the matter. "Please tell me what she needs to defend me from?" Mark voice was quiet, all humor gone. "And why is Jack outside my room? Are you keeping someone out or keeping me in?"

Donovan told him the facts of the case.

Some things Mark knew from Robin and Peter, but it sounded so much worse all put together. It appeared someone had gone to a lot of trouble to set him up. First disbelief, then anger, and finally sadness washed over him. "Chief, someone's setting me up. One of my friends is setting me up." He paused, feeling the hurt of betrayal in his gut. "There's no way around it. I have to remember what happened before they succeed."

~*~

Oscar waited in his car. He'd gotten the word he was supposed to do the job on the cop tonight. Apparently, the guy was awake, and Carlo didn't want to take any chances. He snorted. Carlo didn't want to take chances, but it was OK if Oscar did.

Why had they waited so long, and how would he make it happen? Killing a cop! And a guarded cop at that! What was Carlo thinking? He simply said to show up tonight by eleven and the guard wouldn't be a problem. He hoped not, because Colorado still had the death penalty, and killing a cop would guarantee it. If he wasn't shot first. He transferred the gun from the glove compartment to his pocket. At least if he did this, he'd have a chance at getting away. Telling these people no wasn't an option; it was suicide.

He waited until the cop's wife headed for her car before he left the parking lot. Good, he still had plenty of time. He strolled in the emergency entrance and rode the elevator to the second floor, the same way he'd practiced it. He then dashed up two flights of stairs and peered through the little glass square in the door. The hallway was clear. He crouched and eased open the door.

The stairs, close to the end of the hall, offered a view of the whole corridor. A couple of empty rooms yawned in front of him. And down the hall, like the other night, sat the guard, lounging in the chair reading a magazine. A nurse came by and refilled his coffee, her body language flirty. The cop beamed as she moved away.

The elevator dinged. A man exited and headed for the guarded room. He stopped to talk to the cop then entered. Oh, great, extra company. That's all he needed—more people in the room. What would he do now?

What choice did he have but to wait? Maybe the guy wouldn't stay long. He eased through the door and settled into a shadowy doorway. Kind of late for visitors, wasn't it?

Could be a doctor, but he didn't have a white coat. The man came back out after about thirty minutes. As he walked toward the elevator, Oscar studied him. The chief of police. No wonder he didn't wait for visiting hours and passed the cop with such ease. Oscar shrank deeper into the doorway.

As soon as the chief entered the elevator, the guard went into the room. Why? Was there something wrong with the cop? Maybe he'd croak on his own, and Oscar wouldn't have to lift a finger. Wouldn't that be a relief?

He checked his watch. Ten forty-five. Did that mean the guard was out of the picture? Was someone already in the room when he'd gotten here? And if so, why didn't they kill Clayton while they were at it? Should he come out now or wait?

The nurse came by again, set a full cup of coffee on the floor, and retrieved the other one. Boy, the service in this place was great if one was a cop. Bet if he was in here, there wouldn't be sweet-looking nurses tripping over themselves to get him coffee.

The guard came back out and sat. He grinned when he saw the full cup of coffee, picked it up, and drank a few sips.

Oscar checked his watch again. Almost eleven. What kind of diversion had they planned to draw the cop away? And when would it happen?

The cop slumped against the wall. Steaming coffee spilled down his leg onto the floor. Nobody could sleep through that. He must be out cold.

Oscar leapt out, made sure no one was coming, and hurried to the sleeping cop. He prodded him, almost knocking him off the chair. "Hey, officer, you awake?"

No response. He pushed the door open and went inside.

25

Peter drove Libby's SUV into the hospital parking lot. It was late, almost eleven o'clock. He'd gotten tied up at dinner with Libby's family and didn't realize the passing time. He dropped her off at home and came straight over. It was probably too late, but he wanted to ask Mark about little Joey while the questions were fresh in his head. He parked and then hesitated. If Mark was sleeping, he didn't want to disturb him. It could wait 'til tomorrow, but maybe he was up.

He pulled his phone out of the holder and struggled to find Mark's new number. "I'm downstairs. You awake?" He texted.

His phone binged back. "Sure, come on up."

Chief Donovan was in the lobby heading out. "Hey, what are you doing here so late? Do you have news?"

Peter told him about his interview with Timmy. "I just wanted to see if he remembered anything more about Joey. It could wait, but it's bugging me. I texted Mark, and he's still awake. You want to go up with me?"

Donovan shrugged. "Might as well. I'd like to hear what he has to say. I never got the chance to talk to Joey, and it's always bothered me."

Upstairs, Peter stepped out of the elevator and froze. Jack was asleep on duty.

"Jack!" he barked.

No response. His heart pounding, he pulled his gun from his shoulder holster. Horrifying images flooded his mind as he slammed through the door, hitting something hard on the other side. The tang of gunpowder assaulted his nostrils, but he hadn't heard a shot. Was he too late?

"Police, drop it!" He screamed as a man stumbled and then stood up. He wasn't tall, but solidly built. Donovan pushed in behind Peter. The man dropped his weapon, put his hands in the air, and faced them. Donovan moved around Peter and kicked the gun out of the way.

A silencer. Peter's breath caught. No wonder he hadn't heard the shot. He glanced quickly at the bed. It was empty.

A nurse skidded into the room, missing him by inches, and halted at the sight of a gun in his hand.

A second nurse yelled, trying to rouse Jack.

"Chief! What's going on?" the first nurse asked. "Where's the patient?"

"Under here." Mark slid out from under the bed.

The nurse who'd first entered moved to help him up. She reached over and shut off the machine next to the bed, which until then, Peter hadn't noticed had been screaming. In the ensuing silence, they could hear someone in the hall calling for a stretcher.

"Turn around and face the wall," Donovan said. "Now don't start anything, or Detective Fox will shoot you." While Peter kept him covered, Donovan pushed the man's face into the wall, patted him down, and cuffed him.

The nurse tried to help Mark back into bed. Mark resisted. "Wait. Is Jack OK? What happened to him?"

"Get into bed, and I'll find out." By the determination on her face, she wasn't moving until he did.

"Do as she says, Mark, I don't need another officer down. Oh, and call the station, would you?"

Mark grinned and perched on the edge of the bed. "There. Are you happy?" he said to the nurse as he reached for his cell phone.

She stood her ground until satisfied he would stay and, nodding once, scooted into the hall. In a few minutes, she was back.

"Your friend is OK. Drugged, I'd say. His vitals are good, so he's being moved to another room to recover." She plucked the dangling monitor wires off the floor and approached Mark. "You need to get into bed, so I can hook you back up."

"No," Donovan interrupted. "He won't be staying."

"What?" She dropped her jaw. She stood holding the wires. "He can't go anywhere. He hasn't been discharged."

Peter almost laughed.

"I think maybe he has." Donovan stuck two fingers into his prisoner's back pocket and slid a wallet out. He casually leaned against the wall and flipped it open. To the nurse, he said, "Can you bring a doctor in here, please?"

The nurse spun and left the room.

"You can turn around now." The man faced them, and for the first time, Peter got a good look at him. Perhaps in his late thirties, his pale skin contrasted with dark brown hair and eyes.

"Do either of you know who this guy is?" Donovan asked.

"No, sir. I've never seen him before," Mark said.

Peter kept his gaze, and his gun, on the suspect. "Me, either."

Donovan tossed the wallet on the bed. "Mr. Russo, why did you try to shoot Detective Clayton?"

The man stared at the gun still pointed at his chest and didn't answer.

Mark finished his call and flipped open the wallet. "Oscar Russo. I don't know an Oscar Russo."

"Mr. Russo, you're mighty lucky you didn't get the job done. You'd better hope the other officer wasn't harmed."

Oscar opened his mouth, so Donovan paused. The moment passed, and Oscar clamped it shut.

"Did someone hire you to do this?"

Oscar lowered his gaze.

Donovan leaned against the bed, his gun not wavering. "So, it was a hit." He glared at Oscar. "Was this your first one?"

No answer.

Donovan smirked. "Did anyone ever tell you, you might not be cut out for this line of work?"

Mark and Peter laughed.

The man's face reddened, but still he kept silent.

Ten minutes passed before the elevator dinged. The sound of an army of footsteps rang in the hall. Evans and Rodriguez escorted Oscar out. Anderson took Jack's place at the door, and Daniels waited in Mark's room.

After handing over his prisoner, Peter left the room to check on Jack. He was still out.

Walking down the hall, Peter searched the rooms at the end of the hall. Still empty, no other threats remained. He continued to the stairwell and stepped through the door, his gaze sweeping up and down the steps.

He heard Donovan on the phone. "I need a favor," he said.

Peter returned to Mark's room in time to hear Daniels taking Mark's statement.

Dr. Zimmerman was waiting. "I hear we've had some excitement tonight."

Donovan came back in the room. "I didn't realize they would get you out of bed. I expected to get the doctor on call."

He laughed. "Nurse Ryan knows to call me if something critical happens involving one of my patients. I've examined Mark, and he's doing fine. I don't think this will affect his recovery." He started to go.

"Wait, doc. I'm taking him out of here."

The doctor stopped. He didn't say anything at first but then swiveled. "I guess I can see the wisdom in that. I was going to release him tomorrow anyway." He scanned Mark. "Where do you want me to call in your prescription?"

Mark glanced up at Donovan. "Just write a script, would you, Doc?"

Zimmerman nodded. "Of course. I'll be right back."

When he was gone, Peter sat next to the bed. Sitting felt good, even if just for a minute. "I think you scared Nurse Ryan to death, pulling your monitor wires off, Mark. Good thinking. It certainly got her attention. Now, tell us what happened."

Mark leaned back on his pillows. "After you left, Chief, Jack came in to use the bathroom. We talked for a second, and then he went into the hall. I got your text, Peter, so when I heard the handle click I thought it was you. Instead, this man came in and fiddled with his jacket." Mark took a breath. "I don't know why, but it spooked me. I rolled off the bed, and something hit my pillow. I scooted under and yanked the cords off my chest, mostly to get them out of the way, and I was kind of hoping someone would notice." He grinned. "He must have been heading around to the side of the bed when you came in and hit him with the door. What made you come? I'm glad you did, but why? Did you suspect something?"

"No, nothing so complicated." Peter chuckled. "I wanted to talk to you about Joey. We can do it later though."

Donovan went to the door and opened it. "Peter, help him get dressed. Mark, you'll be safer if you're out of here before anyone knows you're gone."

26

Peter didn't ask where they were going, although he was dying to know. The chief wasn't in the mood to elaborate, so he'd find out soon enough.

Mark struggled into some pants, still wearing the hospital gown.

"Where's your shirt?" Peter asked. Then he remembered it was probably being tested for gun residue.

"It's gone. Probably wasn't wearable anyway."

Peter pictured a shirt soaked with blood. "You'll just have to wear the gown for now. I can get you some clothes later."

Mark switched the gown around so the opening was in the front, and tucked the bottom half into his pants. "This'll have to do. Any idea where we're going?"

"Not a clue. I don't think we'll know 'til we get there." Peter grabbed the rest of Mark's belongings, threw Mark's coat over his shoulders, and hurried him out a door at the back of the hospital.

The chief helped load him into the SUV then led in his own. Peter finally had a chance to think. These people must be crazy. What kind of desperation did it take to walk right into a guarded room and kill a cop?

Donovan drove high and deep into the mountains, the roads so twisting Peter couldn't have found his own way back. Good thing Libby had GPS; he'd need it. He glanced over.

Mark was asleep, his jaw slack, features drained of tension. Good. The more rest he got, the better.

The chief slowed onto a dirt road and followed it for a couple of miles before turning onto a narrower dirt road, which ended up being a driveway.

Mark opened his eyes when they parked behind Donovan. "Where are we?"

"I have no idea." Peter rolled the window down as Donovan got out of his vehicle. "Is this yours? I didn't know you had a cabin."

"It belongs to a friend of mine." Donovan opened Mark's door and helped him out. "He's meeting us here."

An old blue pickup glinted in the porch light. The front door opened, and a big man, with an even bigger smile, lumbered out. "Welcome. Come on in."

"Lenny, meet Mark and Peter. Guys, this is one of my oldest and best friends."

Lenny hefted a cooler out of the pickup. "Hey, watch who you're calling old there, buddy."

Donovan laughed. "Honestly, Lenny, I appreciate this."

"Yes," Mark spoke up. "I can't thank you enough for letting me impose on you this way."

"It's not an imposition. Pat Donovan's friends are always welcome here." Lenny ushered them into a cozy living room with a roaring fire.

"You must have gotten here fast," the chief said.

"It didn't take me long to find a replacement at the center. So all I had to do was stop for provisions and head on up. I know it's early for breakfast, but how about some flapjacks?"

Peter's mouth watered. "How can I help?"

"You can get us some orange juice and set the table. I keep some stuff here, so I don't have to haul it back and forth." He pulled out a skillet and placed it on the stove. "Pat, do you want breakfast before you head back?"

Peter faced the chief. "Are you going back tonight?"

"Yeah, but breakfast sounds too good to miss."

Flapjacks became more than pancakes and included bacon, eggs, and toast.

Peter scooted away from the table stuffed, and by the look of it, so was everyone else.

Mark placed both hands on his stomach. "Man, that tasted good. Much better than the hospital food I've had the last couple of days."

Lenny, sopping up syrup with a corner of toast, jerked his attention from his now-clean plate. "I hope I didn't feed you anything you weren't supposed to eat."

Mark grinned. "Well, I ate it, so it's my own fault if it comes back up. But I don't think it will. I feel pretty good right now."

Lenny rose to clear the table, and they all jumped up to help. "Pat, you'd better get on down the road. Don't worry about this. We've got it."

The rustic log cabin offered no dishwasher. Peter searched the cabinet for dish soap and filled the sink while Lenny scraped crumbs into the trash and set it next to the door. "I'll take that down with me when I leave."

Mark carried dishes to the sink, but with one good arm, it wasn't going fast. He glanced at Lenny. "Take it where?"

Lenny grabbed a towel and started drying. "A garbage facility in town."

Mark laughed. "No home pickup here, eh?"

Lenny stacked the plates. "If you put it outside, the bears get it. Then they know they can find food in the cabins. Not a good idea. We're required to use the bear-proof containers in town. There's a hefty fine if they catch you putting your trash outside."

Clinking silverware rattled in the sink. Were there bears outside? Peter cringed. At least he had his gun. Although, wouldn't a bullet just make a bear mad?

Better think of something else. "How do you know the chief, Lenny? Sounds like you're pretty good friends."

"We are. We were partners in Denver many years ago. I wouldn't be here if it weren't for Pat Donovan."

"What happened?"

"We were called to a possible domestic dispute. A neighbor heard a man screaming at his wife and thought she heard him threaten to kill her. He had a history of slapping her around, so the neighbor worried. The guy let us in, and when we asked to see her, he said she left." Lenny paused with a plate in his hand and leaned against the counter. "You should have seen the place. It was trashed—broken glass all over the floor, pictures hanging sideways on the walls, and a lamp lying in pieces in the corner. Pat looked at me and I looked at him, and we advanced toward that bedroom door." Lenny placed the dry plate on the stack.

Mark stopped wiping the table.

Peter turned to listen, sponge resting on the half-clean glass in his hand.

"He started yelling about what we were doing,

asking us if we had a warrant, screaming we couldn't go in there. Pat didn't like the fact that he was yelling. Later, he said it seemed like the guy was trying to warn someone. Anyway, we got to the door, and Pat yanked me sideways just as a bullet splintered the wood, right where I would've been standing. The guy who answered the door wasn't the homeowner. He was the shooter's brother."

Mark resumed wiping the table.

Peter released a breath. He finished the glass and set it on the counter.

"The brother lived in the basement and came up when he heard a gunshot. The husband confessed to shooting his wife when he found out she was pregnant with another man's child." Lenny shook his head. "What a mess. Domestics are the worst." He slid the stack of plates in a cabinet. "So that's how he saved my life. We've been pretty tight ever since. He thinks it was a reflex, but I know it was God."

Peter was sure he was right. He finished the dishes, pulled the plug, and let water run out of the sink. Lenny seemed to come back from wherever the memory had taken him. "Enough talk. We need to get you to bed, Mark. You look half dead, pardon the expression."

And he did. A strong wind would knock Mark over. He almost swayed on his feet. Lenny made Mark sit while he threw some sheets on a bed in one of the bedrooms. Mark said good night, went in, and closed the door.

Peter was so tired he thought he could sleep standing up, but he found the energy to fight with Lenny over taking the couch. Still, Peter lost the argument.

27

Robin hung up the phone with a shaky hand. Only two o'clock, but no way could she go back to sleep now. How could this happen? How did they get to Mark through a police guard? She wrapped her robe tight and splashed some water on her face. Should she wake Mark's parents or let them sleep and tell them later?

Ed stood in the hall outside the guest room door, saving her the decision. Eyes hooded, he held the banister as if bracing for bad news. "Was that the hospital? Is Mark all right?"

"That was Mark, actually," she spoke quickly to calm him.

Ed released a breath and eased his death-grip on the banister. Standing there in his PJs, he seemed frail. This must be such a strain for him. *Please, God, don't let him have a heart attack. And give me the best way to tell him.* He wouldn't thank her for shielding him. "Mark's fine, but they've moved him somewhere else. There was an attempt on his life."

Ed inhaled another sharp breath and blanched.

Silvia's exclamation burst from the bedroom—not a word, but a sound deep in her throat. The door opened wider, and she peered out.

"It appears someone drugged Jack's coffee and went into Mark's room and shot at him," Robin said.

"God saved him in the form of Peter and Chief Donovan." She cleared her throat. "They have the guy in custody, but the chief didn't want to leave Mark there."

Silvia stepped out.

"Where did they take him?" Ed asked.

"He called from the hospital. He didn't know where he was going, but he said he was fine and not to worry. He sounded tired but promised he was unhurt. All I know is Peter is with him."

They headed downstairs for tea and toast, none able to go back to bed.

After breakfast, she proceeded to her home office and sighed at all the stuff on her desk. She checked her watch. Concentrating on work might get her through the next hours until she could call Libby. Once Libby's kids left for school, Libby might have some time to talk. She'd try her cell phone. Maybe Peter told her something Mark missed.

She worked until seven thirty, cleaning her desk and organizing what had piled there all week. Then she let her muscles relax in a warm shower, the heat calming her. At least this eliminated Chief Donovan from her suspects. After all, it couldn't be him, not since he'd saved Mark's life. Although wouldn't that be the perfect way to get to Mark? Move him from the hospital to who knows where? *No. Don't even think it.* Peter was with him, and she trusted Peter.

She finished her shower, called good-bye to her in-laws, and left. Maggie's was on the way. Robin had filled her in on the phone, and she'd agreed to come along. When they arrived, Libby ushered them inside, a full pot of coffee waiting. Robin tucked one foot under her as she sat at the round kitchen table. "Don't keep me in suspense. What do you know?"

Libby handed her coffee. "I don't know any more than you do. Peter left for the hospital late last night, wanting to talk to Mark. He called telling me someone tried to kill Mark and they were moving him. Peter is staying with Mark and won't be home for a few days."

Robin blew on her coffee. "Did he say where they were taking him?"

Libby poured a cup for Maggie and then one for herself. "He didn't know. Someplace the chief picked out."

Robin curled her hands around her cup for warmth. "Is that all he said? He didn't say how they were protecting him?"

Libby tipped some milk into her cup. "No, honey, he didn't. When Mark called, was he on his cell phone?"

"Yeah. He said he was turning it off so I wouldn't be able to reach him." How could they just sit here drinking coffee while Mark was in danger? But then what else could they do?

Libby splashed in more milk, took another sip, and nodded. "What exactly did he tell you?"

"Not much. He said someone shot at him, but he was all right. They caught the guy, but the chief doesn't want to take any chances." She lifted her gaze to her friend's face. "Libby, what if they can't protect him?"

Libby gave her hand a squeeze and sat back. "I'm sure he's all right. If the chief isn't telling anyone but Peter, then you know he's taking every precaution."

Robin twisted her hands. "The problem is, if they're both guarding Mark, and they don't trust anyone else, who's looking for the killer?"

28

Oscar stared at the cinderblock wall of his jail cell. The white paint was peeling in some places. His fingers itched to pick at it. How long would it take before he got his phone call? Maybe he wouldn't get one. Trying to kill a cop, he was lucky no one had touched him yet. The chief was known as a straight arrow though, so they probably didn't have brutality with him in charge.

He was going to prison. No way he'd rat out the others. Not that he wouldn't like to. At least to enlighten the cops about Carlo, the little weasel. It was a bad plan, and he knew it. Had he wanted Oscar to get caught? What kind of game was he playing?

Bad plan or not, nobody said no to Carlo. People didn't live long who tried. Somebody needed to take him out, and someday somebody would. Too bad he wouldn't be there to see it. He'd face twenty years once they figured out how many charges they could rack up. And the guard. What did the girl do to him? If he died, it would be a murder rap. He'd never see the light of day, even though it wasn't him that done it.

Hours passed before someone came to get him. Two people, a dark-haired guy and a blonde took him to a room, read him his rights, and began to question him. They probably said their names, but he couldn't remember.

The guy asked his name and address for the record. A recorder purred on the table. He answered the questions—after all, they had his wallet with his driver's license.

Then the guy got serious. "Who paid you to kill Mark Clayton?"

Oscar said nothing.

"Did you know he's a cop?"

Nothing.

"It won't help you to protect them, you know. They wouldn't if it was them in here," the blonde chirped.

She was right, but he made his face into stone. They could try to make him talk, but he was tough. He'd wait it out. Sooner or later, they'd have to let him go back to his cell. She placed her elbows on the table. "So, Oscar, how about the green sedan in your garage? Is it yours?"

He should have known they'd check his place out before questioning him.

"You know we're adding another attempted murder to your sheet, don't you?"

"I didn't try to kill the wife." His voice cracked, so he cleared his throat.

"Ah, he speaks." He didn't care if she was attractive; Blondie had an attitude. "So if you didn't try to kill her, what were you trying to do?"

"I just wanted to scare her a little."

"Why? What did she do to you?"

He decided to wipe the smug smile off her face. "She's a cop's wife, that's what. Living high on the hog while other people have to work hard. But I'm not answering no more of your questions."

They screamed and yelled, smiled and coaxed, but

he didn't say another word. When they threatened him, he didn't budge. He shouldn't have talked at all. He was supposed to sit and say nothing. That's what they always tell you: "Don't say nothing." But it kind of made him mad. If he'd been trying to kill her, she'd be dead. And if those cops hadn't come in, Clayton would be dead, too, and none of this would be happening.

No more boring drives following that stupid lady and no more worrying about how he could kill a cop. Getting caught was almost a relief. At least he didn't have to worry about Carlo now. Unless he squealed. Then whoever they had on the force would turn him in, and Carlo would find a way to get him. Even in here.

~*~

Peter sat up, startled. Already nine o'clock. The plan was to sleep for three hours and wake at seven, but the five hours he got felt great. Someone was moving in the kitchen.

Mark turned around when he came in. "Hey, good morning. I was getting some breakfast. Do you want some?"

"Sure, sounds great, but I'll make it. Where's Lenny? The couch is mysteriously empty."

Mark slouched into a chair and exhaled. "I can't believe you let him sleep on the couch."

Peter rummaged through the cabinets for oatmeal. "Let him? I argued, but does anyone win an argument with him?"

"I doubt it." Mark laughed.

Hearing it sounded so good. A week ago they'd feared he wouldn't make it, and now he was laughing as if he didn't have a care in the world.

"He went out for more supplies," Mark said. "He's picking up a new shirt for me, thank heavens. He lent me one of his, but…" He lifted his good arm. The sleeve stopped mid forearm. "Also, he's getting more groceries. I told him I thought it would be a couple days at the most."

Peter stopped midstride, holding the oatmeal in the air. "Why? What happened?"

Mark grinned. "I'm beginning to remember."

29

Tony woke up thinking about Lucy. She'd called and let him know Mark was awake, but they'd made no plans to see him yet. Tony hoped it'd be soon. He wanted to see Lucy, but he also liked the idea of visiting Mark. He was a nice guy, and all the youth group kids liked him. He picked up his phone to check the weather. It was supposed to hit sixty today. He grabbed some jeans and a t-shirt and hopped into the shower.

Downstairs, Dad sat at the kitchen table munching on some toast.

"Where's Mom?"

"She's still getting ready."

Uh-oh. If Mom was in her room, and Dad was eating toast for breakfast, they were probably fighting again. She would stay in there until Dad left, or she'd get ready and leave without him. Tony grabbed a cereal bar, waved at his dad, and headed out the door. He'd be late for his first class if he didn't hurry.

The radio was giving the weather report. Yep, sixty, just like his phone. Once the news came on he changed the station. What was that? Did he hear the name Oscar Russo? He changed it back.

"...Detective Mark Clayton, recovering at Good Samaritan Hospital after having been shot at a warehouse during a drug bust last week, sources say.

More after this."

What? Was this another report about Mark? He was sure he heard Oscar Russo's name. That was the guy at the meeting. Whatever it was, he'd missed it, and he didn't have time to wait through the commercials. He needed to get to class. Mrs. Lindon was a stickler about tardiness.

Once inside his first period, he eased his phone out of his pocket, his eyes on the teacher. She got pretty mad if you had your cell phone out in class, and he'd lose it if she saw him with it.

She didn't give him any opportunity to check out the news story but started right in on last night's homework. He pushed the phone back in his pocket and took his notebook out of his backpack. It would have to wait until after class.

Fifty minutes later, he placed his book in his backpack, swung it over his shoulder, and grabbed his phone. He could catch the news story on his way to American History. He scanned his newsfeed. The headline, "Is Our Town Safe?" caught his eye. He stopped in the hallway, causing a girl to run into him.

"Hey, watch it," she said.

"Sorry," he mumbled.

He started forward again, still reading. "In a daring display, a man identified as Oscar Russo shot at Detective Mark Clayton last night at Good Samaritan Hospital." Tony continued to the end of the article. What? Someone tried to kill Mark again? And they think it was Oscar? He remembered the guy from the meeting. They must have made a mistake. He went on to class, but he couldn't concentrate.

The teacher called on him, and he had no idea what the man said.

"Sleepy today, Mr. Rosetti?"

Tony's face warmed. Thankfully, he moved on to another student. Tony tried to focus on the civil war, normally an interesting subject for him, but he couldn't. All he could think about was that meeting. All that talk about oregano. Oscar not wanting to 'remove the impediment to our distribution.'

Tony remembered his words exactly. He also remembered his dad's reaction. It didn't have anything to do with oregano. They were talking murder. And Oscar tried to carry it out. It must be some kind of joke. Deep in his gut, he didn't think so.

If someone tried to kill Mark during a possible drug bust, they must be involved in drugs, right? Could that be the 'oregano' they kept talking about? Tony's face flamed. How stupid could he get? All that time he thought they were discussing spaghetti spices, but they were really talking about drugs? He had to get to the restaurant. Dad would have to tell him the truth.

30

Robin sat straight and gripped the armrest on the door of Maggie's car, her palms sweating. They were going to accuse a police officer of selling drugs. How did a person do something like that?

She was about to find out, because Maggie was on a mission, and she couldn't let her go alone. She glanced at Maggie's profile. Her face was pale but set, as she rounded the corner onto Greg's street. Robin should never have told her about Greg's past. She should have asked Peter to check it out instead. But Maggie really liked this guy. She was determined to find out if he was dirty.

They approached a park near Greg's house. "Stop here for a minute. I want to make sure we have some kind of plan before we barge in accusing Greg."

Maggie drove into the adjacent lot and pulled into a space, leaving the engine running. Brow lifted, she turned to Robin and waited.

Robin tugged at the sash of her seatbelt. Why was it so claustrophobic in here? "What did we learn from our drive around yesterday?"

Maggie stayed quiet, so Robin continued.

"I think we cleared Tammi." Robin tapped the armrest. "She and her mom don't get along. When she married Ron, her mom told her she was making a mistake. She's been saying 'I told you so' ever since. If she's having her come to live with them, then Tammi's desperate and has to think there's no other way. Her mom is great with Tisha but hard on Tammi. If she had money from another source, she wouldn't put herself through it. If we can clear Greg today, then that's two down."

"I'm not sure we've cleared Tammi, but it doesn't appear she's expecting a windfall. And even if we hear what we want to hear from Greg, can we say that makes him innocent?" Maggie loosened her grip on the wheel. "He won't fall on his knees and tell us he did it and beg our forgiveness. Whatever he tells us, we still won't know if it's the truth."

Robin stared out at the kids playing on the swings. "I guess you're right. Are you sure you want to do this?"

"No, but I have to know." She turned back onto Greg's street, and scowled at his building as it came into view. She parked.

Robin reached for the door handle. "I'm glad it's his day off. We don't have to go to the station to talk to him."

"Not Sunday? I would've thought, being a churchgoer, Greg would want Sundays off."

"I asked him once." Robin swung open the door and stepped out. "He said he wanted to give people with families a chance to take their kids to church."

Maggie followed her up the walk. "Doesn't sound much like a drug dealer to me."

Robin got off the elevator and knocked on Greg's door. Her heart pounded as she dried her hands on her jeans. Maybe he wouldn't be home, and they could wait until later.

As she peeked at the elevator behind her and

edged toward it, Greg answered the door. His gaze fell on Maggie, and his smile spread. Then he glanced at Robin. His expression fell and tightened. "What happened? Did someone send you to get me? I didn't get a call. At least I think my phone is working." He yanked his phone off his belt and checked it.

Robin gaped at him. What was—he hadn't heard from the station. He didn't know what happened to Mark. Or if he did, he wasn't sharing it with them.

Maggie stood there like a stone. So much for being so determined to know.

Robin almost scoffed. "Someone made an attempt on Mark's life last night, but that's not why we're here."Greg's face registered shock, so she told him what she knew about the attack.

"Is he OK? I'd better get to the station and see what's going on." He patted his pockets. "I can't believe no one called me."

Maggie assured him Mark was OK and took a deep breath. "I'd better get down to why we're here. We wanted to ask you a few questions. Robin's going out of her mind with worry, and since Mark is hidden away for now, we're checking out a few things ourselves."

That's great. Blame me why don't you?

Greg led them into what he called the den. Book-laden shelves flanked a cozy fireplace. The massive mahogany desk dominating one corner might have qualified it as a home office, except the spacious room still contained a full set of living room furniture. "Come in and make yourself at home. Stinky, get out of the way."

A white Persian leapt from the leather couch and pranced out of the room, her beautiful head high and her tail waving.

"That name definitely does not match the cat." Maggie laughed as she sat on the couch.

"How did she get it?" Robin claimed the place next to Maggie. There was strength in numbers, right?

Greg relaxed into a lumpy recliner and kicked one foot across his other knee. "When she was a kitten, she happened to be in the vicinity when the neighbor's dog found a skunk. She got caught in the crossfire. My niece named her Stinky because she stank for weeks. Now I call her it to annoy her. I think she knows what it means. Most of the time, I call her Snowball, which also seems to annoy her. But then everything I do annoys her. Now, how can I annoy...I mean help...you?" He smiled at Maggie.

Robin could tell she was taking in all that dark hair, and those gorgeous blue eyes. Robin had to admit, he really was a hunk. How was it that he wasn't married? Handsome, charming, rich...no wonder Maggie was attracted.

Robin clasped her hands to stop their trembling and placed them in her lap. "I wanted to ask if you remember the day before Mark got shot. Did he say anything strange to you?"

"Strange how?"

"I don't know...anything. We don't know what we're looking for. But we're hoping someone will remember something to make sense out of him going to an abandoned warehouse at six in the morning."

"No, he didn't say anything to me, and if he had, I would've already started working on it." He narrowed his eyes. "What are you guys up to? You know we've already covered this over and over. Whatever you've came to ask, just ask."

Maggie plunged ahead. "We came to talk to you about a mysterious trip the summer of your fifteenth year."

"What? What are you talking about? What mysterious trip?"

Robin shrank a little. "Some people remembered you got into trouble and your father sent you away."

He frowned, and the warmth fled from his eyes.

Why had they come? This wasn't a good idea.

He leaned back. "I'm sure 'some people' have their own ideas about that. Why don't you ask them?"

Maggie scooted forward. "Because we wanted to ask you. They think it was drugs, and we thought it fair to find out for ourselves."

"It was foolish is what it was." His voice rose. "Do you think I'm behind all this? Do you realize that if I am, you two are in serious danger?" He sprang from his chair.

A tremor skittered down Robin's spine.

Maggie must have felt it too because she shrank farther into the couch.

He didn't come near them but began to pace. "Have you been going around asking other people these kinds of questions? You could get yourselves killed."

Robin held her breath, afraid but not wanting to leave without an answer.

Maggie's body stiffened.

"Yes, it involved drugs." He lowered his voice. "My father caught a friend and me smoking pot behind the garage and decided to separate me from the kids I'd been running around with. He sent me to my uncle's ranch and told him to work my butt off. My uncle happily obliged because he needed the extra help." He moved toward them, but Maggie didn't flinch or seem to feel any fear. He hooked an ottoman with his foot, dragged it over directly in front of her, and sat.

"I'd never worked so hard in my life, but I loved it. I realized that if you lie down with dogs you're bound to get up with fleas, as my aunt used to say," He searched her face and continued softly, as though speaking only to her. "After the summer, I had a brand-new attitude. The things my old friends did for entertainment weren't so fun anymore. I returned every summer until I was out of college."

He shifted toward Robin. "Does Mark think that because my dad caught me with pot twenty years ago I'm a drug addict, or worse, a dealer? Maybe even a murderer?" He looked from Robin to Maggie and back again. "Do you?"

"No, of course not." The heat rose up her face. "Mark doesn't know about this. And we didn't think you were a dealer or a murderer or...I mean we thought maybe you...well..."

"One of the reasons they selected me for the task force was I saw what drugs did to my friends. Years later, one of them died of an overdose." He stood and moved away, his fingers flexing as if he might strangle them if he got too close. "Do you know how dangerous this was? I can't believe you would be so foolhardy as to try to solve this yourself. Do you think you can ask a few questions, and the murderer will come clean? Do you think he'll say, 'Yeah, I did it, but I'm sorry now'?" His voice escalated again.

Robin glanced at the doorway. Too bad she couldn't join the cat. She tried to stem the flow by rising to her feet. "We're sorry. We didn't mean to upset you."

"Upset me?" He actually laughed.

She laughed, too. It sounded ridiculous.Maggie joined in and stood, some of the tension dissipating.

"Before you leave, I need you to promise me you won't do this with anyone else."

The lecture was growing tiresome. "We're not likely to now." Maggie flipped her hair and moved toward the door.

Robin followed.

Greg brought up the rear. "No, I mean it. I know I was kind of hard on you, but honestly, you scared me to death. All I could see was the two of you facing down a murderer."

Maggie turned toward him with her hand on the knob. "Trust me; we won't be doing this again."

Robin apologized a few more times before they got behind the closed elevator doors. They barely looked at each other as they drove away. What total idiots. What if he had been the department leak? Or worse, what if he'd been the one who'd killed Cindy?

Robin felt disgusted with herself. "Of course, the chief knew about his past. He'd checked him out before assigning him to the special unit. Why didn't we talk to him before doing something so dangerous?"

"I wanted to hear it from him," Maggie said. "I wanted to see his face when he told his tale so I'd know if he was lying."

"Well, what do you think?"

"He wasn't."

"I didn't think so either. I hope we didn't ruin your chances with him."

Maggie sniffed. "If we did, they weren't that good."

31

Tony drove around thinking about the news report. Deep inside, he'd always known something was wrong with the other part of the business. Why didn't Mom ever let Dad talk about it if it was on the up and up? Why were there so many secrets? He tightened his grip on the wheel and ground his teeth. He was angry but not shocked. Where did he think all the money came from anyway?

He slammed on the brakes. The briefcase! Who delivers money in a briefcase as a joke? At least he hoped it was money. Oh, no, he hadn't delivered drugs, had he? He never even looked! How could he have been so dumb? Could he be guilty now, too? He had to talk to his dad. Maybe he was completely off base. His dad would probably laugh and clear up the whole thing.

Minutes later, he arrived outside Rossetti's, slammed the car door, and ran inside. His mother flitted around in the dining room, going from table to table greeting the lunch guests. Good. At least she was out of her room. He ran up the stairs and burst into his father's office.

Jimmy stretched out in one of the leather chairs facing Dad's desk. Uncle Sal perched in the other one. "The profits—" Sal jolted. All three heads swiveled Tony's way.

"Sorry. Dad, I have to talk to you."

His dad looked at Uncle Sal, who didn't move. "Would you excuse us a minute please, Sal?"

Sal gave him a dirty look, pushed back his chair with a huff, and sauntered from the room.

Jimmy rose, hands braced on the smooth armrests. "Do you want me to leave, too?"

"No, this concerns you," Tony said.

Shrugging, Jimmy slumped back into the chair.

"So, Tony, what's the problem?" Dad asked.

Tony closed the door and stepped in front of his father's desk. "I want to know what's going on. Did you try to kill that policeman? And is oregano code for drugs?"

Both Dad and Jimmy hesitated. Then they spoke at the same time.

"That's ridiculous." Jimmy said.

"Where did you hear that?" Dad asked.

"We provide a product. It's not our fault who buys it," Jimmy said.

"What? Get real! Where are you selling it? Outside the elementary school?"

"Of course not," Dad soothed. "Jimmy, be quiet."

"I know, Dad. You can stop pretending. I didn't want to believe it at first. But I know you're into something illegal, and somehow learning it's drugs doesn't exactly surprise me."

His father sighed. "We don't handle distribution. We bring it in and sell it to someone else. Like the company we buy coffee from for the restaurant. The coffee company sells it to a distributor who sells it to us, and we make it for our customers. We're the distributor, and we don't sell to kids. We can't help it if kids buy it."

"Is that what you told yourself when the kid died last year?"

"It wasn't our fault. We don't know what he got or how he got it. We didn't give it to him."

Tony wasn't hearing this. He balled his hands into fists. They weren't taking responsibility at all. But then looking back, he realized his dad never took responsibility for things when they went wrong. It was always someone else's fault.

"What happened with Mark? I know him, Dad. He teaches Sunday school, and he's a great guy."

"Listen, Tony, we can't tell you everything. It's better for you if you don't know."

"Don't you think it's kinda late for that?"

"Stay out of it!" Jimmy jumped to his feet and shook a finger at him. "I told Dad I didn't think you should be involved. You've always been a little squealer. You tell anybody about this, and I'll wring your scrawny little neck."

"Now, Jimmy, calm down. Your brother's worried about us," Dad said. Then looking at Tony, he added, "You don't understand, son. I want you to forget all about this. You need to let us handle it."

"Forget it? Let you handle it? Is that what you mean when you tell Mom to let you handle the business side of things? You need to get out of this now before someone else gets hurt. Just quit."

His dad shook his head. "It's not so simple. We're not the only ones involved, and there are reasons we can't quit. But we'll be more careful. You don't have to worry. No one will get in trouble."

Tony uncurled his fingers. "Is it the money? I'll bet if Mom knew what you were doing, she'd tell you the money isn't worth it. I'm going to tell her; she'll make you stop." He ran out of the room and down the stairs expecting to hear his brother pounding after him. He didn't hear anything. His mother wasn't in the dining room, so he went into the kitchen.

She stood, leaning against the counter, giving instructions to the new pastry chef.

Tony paced, waiting for her to finish. Finally, the pastry chef walked away, and Tony sprang forward. "Mom, I need to talk to you."

She gazed into his face and moved to the rear of the kitchen where it was currently quiet. "Tony, what's the matter? You look upset."

"I am upset." He tried to whisper. "I found out Dad and Jimmy are dealing drugs." He didn't know what he was expecting, but it sure wasn't the calm way she stared at him.

"You know about this?" his voice squeaked.

She nodded without speaking.

"Why don't you make them stop? Someone tried to kill a cop, and I think Dad may know something about it." Somewhere he'd stopped whispering.

"Shhh! Keep your voice down. There are things about this you don't understand. You'll have to trust me for now, and I'll talk to you about it later, all right?"

He didn't have much choice. The kitchen was filling with people scurrying to prep for the dinner rush. He'd go home and wait for someone there. Whoever got home first would have some explaining to do.

At almost eleven, the garage door rattled open. Jimmy entered the family room, turned off the TV, and headed for the kitchen.

Tony followed.

"Did Dad send you to talk to me?" Tony flung himself into a chair.

"No, I volunteered." Jimmy's voice was quiet. "I wanted you to understand why we can't stop, and why you have to keep it a secret." His face was stiff, and his hands clenched on the top of the chair he stood behind. He turned it around and straddled it, leaning his forearms against the back and trying to relax.

Whatever it was, it must be bad. Although how could it be worse than drugs? "It's Carlo, isn't it? It's something about Carlo?"

Jimmy jerked, and his eyes widened. "Yeah, he's part of it."

"Are you and Dad afraid of him?"

Even though Tony hadn't meant it as a put down, Jimmy puffed up his chest and scowled. "You don't know him, Tony. If you did, you'd be afraid, too. He's a...a killer."

The hair on Tony's arms stood up. "I already am afraid of him. Do you know for sure?"

"Yes."

So much conviction laced the one word.

"It started when we were in that tiny little place in Louisville, remember? We were contacted and offered money to store some stuff. Dad and Mom were having trouble with the mortgage then, and it looked like the perfect solution. I don't think they planned on doing it forever, just long enough to pay everything off. They raked in a lot of money for no work. Sure, some risk was involved, but the way they handled it, not even that much."

"Where was it hidden? Why didn't I know about it?"

Jimmy's lips curled slightly. "Where was the one

place we were never allowed to go?"

A minute passed before it dawned on him. "The wine cellar? You hid it in the wine cellar?"

"Well, I didn't hide it there. I was a kid then, and I didn't know about it either. But yeah, at first, they hid it in crates with a row of bottles on top. You know the area where the expensive wines were locked up?" He hesitated, and Tony nodded. "It probably housed more cocaine than wine. A special mark on the label identified them. I don't know because Carlo handled it. Then we built this place and branched into bottled spaghetti sauce. Once we had a warehouse, bigger shipments became easier to receive and distribute."

Tony stared at him. "You mean we don't sell Mom's sauce?"

"Yes, of course, we sell her sauce. But we distribute other stuff, too."

Tony pictured a jar full of cocaine. "So why can't we turn Carlo in?"

"Because if he didn't kill us, we'd all go to jail." Jimmy's face blanched the color of chalk. "Because I'd go to jail for murder."

Tony's heart skipped a beat. "Y-you killed someone?"

"No, but I was there, and Carlo made it look like I did." A look crossed his face like he was seeing it all in front of him. He shook his head. "Dad wanted out, and he tried to get Carlo caught when I wasn't around. But Carlo got suspicious and took me with him. I didn't know about Dad, or I wouldn't have gone. I didn't even know what we were supposed to be doing. I went to help with a delivery. Next thing I know there's a bunch of screaming, and a cop's pointing a gun at me telling me to put my hands on the wall. I turned around, and someone shot him. But I don't know who did it. They stuck some money in his pocket to make him look guilty and left. He didn't die in the hospital like they thought he would, so they're still trying to kill him. He saw me there, and Carlo. We heard sirens so we hightailed it." Jimmy got up for some water and gulped it. "I found out later about a woman in the warehouse—although I didn't know it at the time. Carlo asked me to pick up this gun. When I handed it to him, I saw he had gloves on, but I didn't think anything of it. The woman's dead, and my fingerprints are on the gun. A gun Carlo has. And he told Dad he'd turn it in if we don't do what he wants."

Jimmy paused as if waiting for Tony to respond. He didn't know what to say, so he nodded and Jimmy went on. "He doesn't trust either of us, although I don't think he knows for sure that Dad tried to get him arrested. He thinks if he gets you involved, Dad won't sacrifice both sons. Mom's so angry with him for getting you involved, she's not speaking to him. Years ago, she made him promise not to let you know about this part of the business. She was already mad, see, when I started."

"What do you mean getting me involved? Do you mean the briefcase?"

"Yeah. She was suspicious, and Dad had to tell her all about it."

"What was in it?"

"Money from the score where the cop was shot. Dad went ahead because he was afraid Carlo would get one of us killed." Jimmy hit the top of the chair with his fist. "It was so stupid to get involved with these people. They never let you out, and you can't trust what they say."

"Can't we just tell someone? Maybe Mark's wife? I know her. She might help us."

Jimmy's face nearly turned purple. "Haven't you been listening? Carlo has friends everywhere, even in the police force." He swallowed hard and lowered his voice. "He has a contact there who feeds him information about what they're doing. That's how we're able to keep this up."

He rubbed his face with both hands then dropped them to his sides. "I don't want to do this anymore, but I don't know what else to do." He stood as if to leave. "Look at me."

Tony fixed his eyes on his brother's. The irises were so dark they melded with the pupils.

"You have to keep what I've told you a secret. Dad and I don't even talk about it. We do what we're told. You have to promise you won't do anything about this, and you can't tell anyone either. Promise me."

32

Robin spent the night praying God would bring Mark home safely and help them catch Cindy's murderer. She'd prayed practically nothing else for a week. She was almost sick of saying it, and she was sure God was sick of hearing it.

She lay there thinking about approaching Greg and pulling Maggie into the stupid stunt. What an idiotic thing to do. What if she'd gotten one or both of them hurt? Maggie regretted suspecting Greg, but Robin didn't. Her husband was suspected of treachery and murder, why not Greg? But after their interview, she believed him. He was too alive when he recounted his experiences. He'd made an impression on Maggie, too. Her face had changed while he talked, as though all kinds of thoughts were going through her head. After this was over, she'd invite them both to dinner. They'd make a cute couple. Who knows, maybe Greg could get through Maggie's tough shell and let her know God loved her.

She threw the covers off and shuffled in to wash her face. Dark circles ringed the eyes staring back at her in the mirror. She wouldn't be winning any beauty contests today. Wonder where Mark woke this morning? Was he in a nice hotel having room service or one of those fleabag motels with roaches the size of a small car? Or a safe house, whatever that was. She tried to picture him in different surroundings but could only see the hospital room. If only she'd been able to talk to him before he'd left. It wasn't safe, and she didn't want him to risk it, but waiting, wondering if he was alive was agony. How long would he have to stay in hiding? Wherever he was, she prayed God would protect him.

She passed the guestroom door and heard her in-laws stirring. Downstairs she poured a cup of coffee, and the day stretched out in front of her. Normally, work would focus her thoughts, but today, concentration wouldn't come easily. Knowing Mark couldn't call, she checked her phone anyway. Nothing except the saved message from Dr. Tracy's office. If there was an opening, she'd try to get in this morning. She certainly wasn't getting anything done here.

Thankfully, Dr. Tracy had a cancellation and fit her in. What were the odds? Maybe things were looking up.

Then she dialed Libby, who picked up on the first ring. "Have you heard anything?"

"No. You?" Robin asked.

"No."

What had she expected?

"Do you want me to come over?" Libby's voice held compassion.

"No, I have a doctor appointment this morning, but thanks."

"What about lunch? Why don't you come over here after your appointment, and I'll fix us something to eat."

She wondered if she should stay with her in-laws. On second thought, they might want some time alone.

"OK, we can talk about your kids or something, anything to keep my mind occupied. I'll be there by noon, twelve thirty at the latest."

She felt better as she headed to the doctor's office across from the hospital. She almost turned into the hospital entrance from habit. She'd been thinking about Mark, as usual. Staying in hiding probably wasn't doing much for his recovery. But then again, being in the hospital almost got him killed. It would be better if he rested, but knowing Mark, he wouldn't. She prayed again for his safety as she walked into the waiting room.

She signed in, wondering what they needed. If Dr. Tracy was putting her on thyroid medication, why didn't she just phone in a prescription? The nurse called her in and took her weight and blood pressure.

"What is this about?" Robin asked. "Do you need more blood?"

The nurse flipped her chart. "No, but let me put you in a room. Dr. Tracy will be right with you. She wanted to talk to you herself."

Uh oh, what could that mean? Why were they making her wait like this? Why didn't they tell her on the phone? *Lord, please don't let me be sick. I can't take any more. Please, Lord.*

Dr. Tracy tapped on the door and slipped in. "Did the nurse tell you why you're here?"

"No. Is something wrong?" Robin twisted her wedding ring around her finger.

Dr. Tracy beamed. "Nothing that about nine months won't cure. Although with you, I think it will be shorter. Based on what you told the nurse last time, I think it's closer to five or six."

"What?" Robin wasn't tracking. "What about five

months?"

Dr. Tracy smiled into her eyes. "You're pregnant, honey."

"Pregnant?" Joy flooded her mind, her fingers tingled, and tears burned her eyes. "Are...Are you sure?" After all this time could it be? Or was it a gigantic mistake? No, it couldn't be a mistake. That's why she'd been feeling sick. It wasn't nerves. It was a baby. She covered her face with her hands and began to cry in earnest.

The doctor wrapped her arms around her and patted her back. "I'm sure you're pregnant, and I think you're fairly far along. I want to do an exam and an ultrasound and see what's going on in there."

Robin left the office a couple of hours later with a picture of a baby. Their baby. The words sounded foreign in her mind. Three and a half months. She was three and a half months along already! She wanted to sing, to dance, to skip. She'd never gone beyond eight weeks. The doctor said her baby looked healthy, and she saw no reason Robin wouldn't go to term with this one.

She floated to her car. What could she do next? She didn't want to go home. It would be impossible not to tell Silvia, and she wanted Mark to be the first to know. She checked her watch. Still too early to go to Libby's. She tried Mark's cell, but no one picked up. Of course, it would be off. What was she thinking? She quickly hung up. Janice. She could visit Janice. After all, she was right next to the hospital. Perfect timing.

Before she knew what she was doing, she found herself on Mark's floor simply out of habit. She might as well check out his room to see if he left anything behind. The room was clean, the bed made, and nothing under it or on the nightstand. His personal items were gone, even the flowers. Although she had expected as much, she still felt let down. She ambled down the familiar hallway, wondering what floor Janice was on.

"Nurse? Nurse! Come in here. I need you," a petulant male voice called behind her.

She looked around for the nurse he was talking to and then realized he must have meant her.

"Can I help you?" She stuck her head in his door. "I'm not the nurse, but I can find her if you want."

"Oh, it's you. You're the policeman's wife, aren't you? The one who got shot at the other night?"

"Yes, I am. Do you know about that?"

"Only what I heard. It doesn't surprise me it happened to him in here though. The nurses ignore you."

"What do you mean, aren't they helping you?"

"When they decide to answer me, they do. But the night before last, I called and called to the blonde nurse going by. I even stood up to make sure she heard me, but she was too busy flirting with the guard outside your husband's door. She was giving him coffee instead of paying attention to the sick people she's supposed to take care of. And now I need something, and no one's paying any attention to me. Maybe I'm not good looking enough."

Robin tried to get a better description of the nurse who gave coffee to the guard, but he clammed up. Promising to fetch the real nurse, she headed in the direction she'd last seen one.

33

Peter looked up from the papers he and Mark had been studying. "I think we've got her."

"My memory isn't enough. We need to get proof." Mark leaned back, looking exhausted. "Do you think you can convince Donovan to get warrants?" He grabbed the chair arm and tried to hoist himself up one-handed. He grimaced. "Maybe I should go."

"Absolutely not. You're in no condition, and you'll just slow me down." Peter gently pushed his friend back into the chair. "I want you to go to bed immediately. This is no big deal. I'll just meet the chief for lunch and lay it all out. If he needs corroboration, we can give you a call. But seriously, he won't. There's enough here for search warrants, and then we'll have what we need."

Peter grabbed his coat and headed for the door. "I'll call you before the fun stuff begins. I promise. He reached the porch and leaned back inside. "Get some rest so you can join us for the arrests."

He let the door slam without waiting for an answer. Excitement thrummed through his veins. Finally. They still had to clarify a few things, like who actually shot Cindy, but once they rounded everyone up, someone would talk. He'd seen it a million times.

The bright sun caused him to put on his sunglasses as he unclipped his cell phone from his belt.

Donovan answered on the first ring. "Peter! What have you got for me?"

Peter wanted to blurt it out, but he'd learned not to ignore the fact that someone could be listening. "Why don't we meet for lunch and we can discuss it?"

"Is it important?" Donovan's voice crackled through static.

"I have something I want you to see."

"Where do you... meet?" The static grew worse. "Call...parking," was all he made out.

"I'll call you back," he found himself yelling. He waited a few minutes for Donovan to get out of the building. Then he called him back.

"So, what's up?" The crackle was less noticeable out here.

Peter sighed with relief. He didn't want to go all the way to the station, and he didn't want the chief to be overheard talking to him. The diner, a small place halfway out of the mountain range where the cabin was located, would be a safe meeting place. "I have something I want to show you. Can you meet me at the diner?"

"Sure. I'll see you there."

Donovan sounded a little strange. Had he already found out? Hope flickered in his psyche. *Don't get too excited*. Probably the bad connection.

When he entered the diner, the place was crowded. His gaze roamed the tables. There. Donovan waved from a booth in the back.

He passed two servers with bright red lipstick, dressed in fifties costumes. Dodging a child in the middle of the aisle, he finally slid into the booth across from his boss.

"Before you tell me why I'm here, I wanted to let

you know we found the green sedan," Donovan said.

"We did? Great! Where was it? Have they traced the owner?"

"It was in the perp's garage."

"You mean the guy from the other night?"

"Yeah. He must have followed Robin home and wanted to scare her. I think he's been keeping tabs on her since then, too, but in a different car. When we searched his place, we found what we think was part of the hit money locked in the glove compartment. The car has dents in the right places as well." He sat back and crossed his legs at the ankles. "Now, why don't you tell me why you dragged me out here?"

Peter pulled his silverware out of a paper napkin and placed them on the table. Now that the time had come, he was nervous. Would he believe him? He saw the naked hope in the chief's eyes. "Chief, I think the informant is Beth."

The hope flickered and died. Peter could almost read the chief's mind. Coming out here—what a waste of time.

"It's not Beth." Donovan's shoulders sagged. "I've known her for years. I would have noticed."

The server showed up with water.

"What led you there?" Donovan asked.

"Her finances. She lives way beyond her means."

"Yeah, but you know why. Janice likes to spoil her. Her house is paid for, her car is paid for, and she has her whole salary to spend on herself. She doesn't need the money." He shook his napkin across his lap. "And I remember seeing some kind of trust or something automatically transfers her money. Remember when we were checking on everyone's finances, we investigated her accounts, and they corresponded with her aunt's."

Peter spread his hands on the table. "We didn't look hard enough. The money for the car did come from Janice's account, but I don't believe Janice signed the check."

The server interrupted to get their order.

Donovan put a hand to his head, as though it hurt. Peter didn't blame him, Beth was the person he trusted the most.

"You'd better start from the beginning." He growled.

Yeah, kill the messenger. Peter swallowed. He had one shot. He'd better make it count.

"Yesterday morning after you left and we got some sleep, Mark started to remember pieces of that day. He and I replayed each step he took. He thought he remembered waiting for backup, and you know it's not like him to go ahead without it. He wasn't sure, but he thought he called it in."

"There were no calls logged from his number. I'm sure you don't think dispatch was involved, too?"

"No. He thinks he called you. Or tried to call you and got Beth. He doesn't remember for sure. It's an impression. She probably promised to get help to him and called someone else instead. When I focused on Beth, it made sense."

Peter stopped for a breath and a sip of water. "I want to investigate, but I'll need your help with additional warrants. I checked on her as much as I could yesterday, and from what I can tell, she was never wealthy. Janice's friends say her niece came and took her away, and they haven't seen much of her since. They say she wasn't sick, but Beth insisted. I find that a little strange, don't you?"

Donovan played with his water glass. "People don't always let their friends and neighbors know how much money they have. And as far as Janice's condition, I'd say she's the type who wouldn't complain. Maybe the friends don't know how bad things were. I'm sure Beth just wanted to keep her aunt safe."

Peter bounced his leg under the table. "I thought so, too, so I called the nursing home. They said before she broke her hip, Janice was fine. They even wondered what she was doing in there. And if we can get her financial information, we might clear this up. If she had the money for years, we should see it."

"OK."

Peter stilled his leg. Was that it?

Donovan pushed the food he'd just been given to the middle of the table.

Peter felt sorry for him. It must be mind-blowing to consider that Beth, his trusted assistant, was listening to everything he said and passing it on.

Donovan couldn't ignore it now though. He had a responsibility to the department to check it out. "I think we can pursue it. Let's go back to the station and question her. If we don't get satisfactory answers, we'll order search warrants."

Peter knew he didn't believe it, but at least he didn't dismiss it out of hand. He took a big bite of his burger. He was starving.

34

After getting Nurse Marlene to check in on the man in 508, Robin went up and down the hall looking for anyone who had seen a blonde nurse. Apparently, both on-duty nurses were brunettes. He could have been mistaken, or it could have been someone with a wig. It didn't necessarily have to be a woman either. It didn't sound like 508 got a good look at her.

It was probably nothing, but Peter or Chief Donovan needed to decide whether to investigate. She dialed Peter and then Chief Donovan, but reached voicemail both times. Leaving messages on both of them, she felt better. On to the reason for her visit. It might even keep her mind off Mark for a little while.

"How are you?"

Janice glanced up with a welcoming smile. "If I was any better, I'd be in Heaven." She pushed the button to raise her bed, and Robin helped her adjust her pillows.

"Now don't be too anxious to go there. We'd miss you too much down here." Didn't she used to go to the community church down on Vine? "So, how's Trinity? Do you still go to church there?"

"The home I'm in has a chapel connected to it, and I go there on Sundays. It's so much easier than trying to catch a bus or beg rides. Sometimes my friends from

Trinity pick me up if there's a special program or something."

Robin smoothed the bedclothes. "I thought Beth went to church with you. Does she come over to the chapel then?"

Janice adjusted her pillows. "I think she's between churches right now. She used to go to Trinity at Christmas and Easter with me, but she's so busy, she hasn't had time."

Robin smiled.

"It's not that she doesn't want to, you know," Janice blurted. "She's busy. In fact, nobody knows how good she is to me, because she won't let me tell anyone. But I don't want you to think badly of her, and I don't think she'd mind if I told you. I know she likes you and Mark."

Beth wore expensive jewelry the other night. You'd think while she was spending Janice's money, she'd at least take her to church. Ouch, that was judgmental. Good job.

"You know she lets people believe my husband's business was successful, and he left me well off. The truth is, although he was a great husband and a second father to Beth, he wasn't a wealthy man. And Beth likes to tell everyone we live off a trust, but it's Beth's money. She pays for it all, even the home I live in." Janice lowered her eyes and picked at the blanket.

"What's the matter? Don't you like the home you're in?"

"Oh, no, I don't mean that. That would be ungrateful!" Distress clouded her face. "It's a lovely place. It really is."

Robin stayed silent and patted her hand.

"The rooms at Sunny View are nice, and the

gardens are beautiful—you should see them in the summer," Janice continued, as though frantic to make her understand. "It's just...I'm not sick. Before I fell and broke my hip, I was as healthy as a horse. And I'm a lot younger than the people there. In fact, that's kind of why I fell." She laughed. "I saw Minnie coming down the hall. She hasn't learned to lean into her walker yet, so she picks it up and swings it when she goes around the corner. I'm not even sure why she has one—I don't think she needs it. But I was trying to get out of her way. I got too close to the edge of the three steps leading to the garden, and I fell off. It was the dumbest thing."

Robin laughed with her, and Beth walked into the room. "You guys seem to be having a good time." She perched on the foot of the bed. "How are you feeling today, sweetheart?"

Janice beamed. "I'm great. The doctor says I can go home soon."

It was time to go. Robin excused herself and headed for the elevator. They had dismissed Beth's high living because of her inheritance. If there was no inheritance, where had she gotten the money? Robin stabbed the down button.

Was Beth the leak? She knew everything Chief Donovan knew, because he trusted her. They'd been working together for years. And she was a blonde. Was she the nurse who gave Jack coffee? Why didn't he recognize her? She obviously didn't pull the trigger because they caught the guy who did. But she knew about it, and if she was the nurse, she had helped.

Beth caught up with her at the elevator and stepped in behind her. A woman stood inside, so Robin and Beth remained silent as they rode down.

Rage at the memory of Beth crying in the waiting room caused her to shake. She would probably have cried at Mark's funeral, too. The elevator descended to the ground floor, and the three of them walked out together. Robin barely contained the force building from her toes and piling up behind her teeth. The woman passed them at the doors leading to the parking lot. Once she got out of earshot, Robin turned.

"You!" She spewed. "You knew someone was trying to kill Mark, and you didn't say a word. In fact, I think you helped them. How could you?"

"I think we'd better go for a drive and talk about this." Beth remained calm.

Robin spun on her heel and pushed through the doors. "I'm not going anywhere with you. I'm going straight to Chief Donovan."

"I don't think so." Beth grabbed her arm and yanked her around. She slid a gun out of her raincoat pocket, hiding it between them. A silencer muzzled the end. "If I shoot you, no one will hear. You'll collapse, and I'll run back in to get help. At least that's how it will look, and I'm pretty good at appearances, aren't I?" Beth smiled, but it didn't reach her eyes.

How had Robin never noticed how cold those blue orbs were? She lowered her gaze and froze, staring at the gun. Beth pushed it into her ribs.

"Walk in front of me. I'll keep it in my pocket. But it's still trained on you, and I will be plenty mad if I have to put a hole in my new coat. It took me forever to find one with pockets this deep." She giggled.

Robin frowned. How had she never noticed the irritating, high-pitched cackling?

She started walking, looking for a way out. She turned left and right and left according to Beth's directions until she spotted the bright yellow sports car. A couple of people stood talking by a car three rows over, but Robin was afraid to call out. What if in trying to save herself she got someone else killed? And what could they do when Beth had a gun? The risk was too great.

The car backed out of its space and left the lot.

Beth unlocked her car with the remote and waited next to the passenger side while Robin opened the door.

"Get in, buckle your seatbelt, and open the glove compartment."

Robin obeyed.

"Now take out the roll of duct tape and tear a large piece off."

Again, Robin complied, biting through the tape, which wasn't easy. Beth had her hold one end in her hand while she took the other end and wrapped it once around her wrists. It went down her hand and around her wrists, and she winced as it pulled at the hair on the back of her arms.

"There. That ought to hold you for a minute." Beth went around the car, watching Robin, and then slid into the driver's seat. She balanced the gun on her lap and wrapped Robin's wrists even tighter.

Beth whisked a cell phone out of nowhere and, still pointing the gun, began to speak, "I'm bringing Mark's wife. It's a long story, and I don't have time. Be there." She ended the call. "Speaking of phones, we'd better take care of yours." She fumbled in Robin's purse, pulled out the phone, and threw it out the window. Another avenue of escape destroyed.

At least Beth hadn't taped her mouth. Robin didn't think she could stand anything over her face.

35

By the time Peter arrived at the station, he could see that Donovan had almost convinced himself it couldn't be Beth.

"This'll make her mad," he said, "but with her and Janice's permission, we can clear it up quickly and move on. We won't have to get any warrants."

Peter hurried to catch up as Donovan snagged Officer Daniels from desk duty to take notes, and then headed upstairs.

Beth wasn't around. There were flowers on her desk, but the picture she had of her aunt was gone.

He had a feeling she wasn't coming back.

Donovan dialed her cell but got no answer. "I can see her with the headset she'd insisted I buy for her a couple years ago when she complained of neck pain. After all, it must have been torture listening to every phone call I made or received. It's a wonder she got any work done."

He jerked open her top desk drawer and rummaged through it. "No wonder she came in early and stayed late. She didn't want to miss anything. I was thinking of giving her a raise!"

Daniels stood at the door with round eyes. "Do you want me to come back later?"

Peter handed him a pad. "Here, take notes of what we're doing and of what we find."

"Everything?" Daniels eyes grew even bigger.

"Everything," the chief replied.

Donovan opened drawers and pulled things out, laying them on the desk. Officer Daniels recorded each thing, personal belongings as well as office supplies. Peter checked the credenza. She didn't have many personal items, some crackers and a couple candy bars. When he got to the third drawer, Donovan stood back. "Here it is."

Peter leaned in. A hole had been drilled in the back of the drawer with a cord threaded through. Nothing was attached to it in the drawer, but the other end ran up to the phone.

Peter didn't know what to say. "I never noticed that her phone had multiple cords."

Finding nothing else, Donovan slammed the drawers shut and sent Officer Daniels to type up the report.

Peter felt a letdown. What could have tipped her off? He concentrated, trying to remember his call. He couldn't remember saying anything that would have given Beth any indication he suspected her. In fact, he was really careful not to. Maybe something in his voice gave him away. Plus, if a person was already suspicious, any small sign could send them running.

Donovan dialed the phone and hit speaker.

"Janice, this is Chief Donovan. How are you?"

"I'm fine, Chief, but if you're looking for Beth, you barely missed them."

"Them? Was she with someone?"

Peter's ears perked up. May she was with her accomplice. If they could catch them together…

"Yes, she and Robin left a little while ago."

"Robin? She was with Robin Clayton?"

"Yes, Robin came to see me, and she and Beth left together."

Donovan hung up, his face ashen.

Peter felt his mouth fall open. "Not Robin," he said. "Not only is she in danger, but now they have leverage. They can try to get Mark out of hiding, and he'll come. As soon as he knows they have Robin, he'll come out."

Donovan held one hand up. "Now let's not jump to conclusions. Maybe her cell isn't working, or she can't hear it. We need to keep trying while we drive to the hospital."

Peter grabbed his keys and sprinted down the stairs. "I should have made her accept police protection." What had he been thinking? She'd convinced him that since she didn't go anywhere but home and the hospital she didn't need it. How could he have been so careless? He would never forgive himself if anything happened to her.

Donovan motioned for Officer Daniels to come along. They sped to the hospital then slowed in the parking lot, watching for either of their cars. They found Robin's, but no sign of Beth's.

Peter and Donovan searched the hospital and had her paged while Daniels waited by her car in case she came out.

Peter headed for the security office to have them check the security tapes, but he had a good idea what they'd find. On his way, he called in an APB for Beth's car.

Donovan waited with him. They leaned over the technician's shoulder and peered at the monitor. There was Robin, leaving the hospital. Beth was behind her.

"Is there another angle?" he asked. "I can't see

Beth's hands."

The technician glanced back apologetically. "Sorry, Chief. This is the only angle."

Peter pointed at the screen. "I think they're in her pockets."

They stopped at Beth's car, and Robin got in the passenger side. Beth's body obscured their view of Robin. Then Beth slammed the door, got in the other side, and drove out of the lot.

Did Beth have a gun? Or did Robin go with her because she didn't sense any danger?

36

Tony stared out the window at blue sky. It promised to be a beautiful day for a drive, although a full retreat was more like what he would do. He carried his bags downstairs and set them by the door. Mom rattled in the kitchen fixing breakfast. He went in and gave her a kiss on the cheek, and she started loading a plate.

Dad was already at the table reading, and apparently, they still weren't talking.

She set Tony's plate on the table and sighed as she sank into the chair across from him. "I want you to call when you get to Grandma Katherine's."

He picked up his fork and ran his thumb along the handle. "I don't want to go. I shouldn't run off when the family needs me."

She rested her hand on his arm. "The mess this family is in isn't your doing." She cast a sideways glance at his dad and, ignoring his grunt, refocused on Tony. "And I want you out of it. When it's safe, you can come home, or we'll join you. Under no circumstances are you to try to fix this on your own. Do you hear me?"

Kind of hard not to. "Yes." Tony stared at his plate. "I'm not a baby, you know, Mom."

She tightened her grip on his arm until he glanced up. Her eyes flashed, and she let go. "There will be no more talk. You will do as I say and go to your grandmother's. Is that clear?"

He nodded. When she spoke like that, there was no use arguing. He wanted to ask where Jimmy was, but she obviously wasn't in the mood.

His dad had lowered the papers he was reading during this whole exchange but hadn't said a word.

And good thing, because Tony could barely keep his mouth shut as it was. He still couldn't believe all this. How could they do something so awful? He wanted to reject the thought. The bad guys Mark had been seeking were under his nose the whole time. At the hospital, Tony even entertained the thought that he, Tony Rossetti, might be the macho man in front of Lucy, solve the case, and save Mark. What a joke! How could Lucy even look at him again?

Even if she didn't know before, it would get around. He'd have to leave home for good. He couldn't face Robin if Mark went to jail for something his father and brother had done, but he couldn't turn his own family in either. Did she already know his family members were suspects? She didn't act like it. And Mark never did either.

Trying to shove it out of his mind, he finished his breakfast, loaded his things in the car, and kissed his mom good-bye. Dad came to the door, but Tony refused to notice him. He slid behind the wheel, backed out, and drove down the street without glancing back.

He wasn't sure when the idea came to him, was it last night or this morning? He would go to his grandmother's but not before uncovering more about Carlo. He was the real bad guy here, and the only way out of this was to get Carlo before Carlo got his family.

He had to be stopped. And obviously neither Dad nor Jimmy would do it.

If he checked out the restaurant, maybe he could catch up with Carlo there. He didn't want to be seen though, so he'd have to be careful. Ignoring what his mother had said, Tony rehearsed his plan. If they were having him followed, it had to appear he was leaving town. He made his way to the highway and headed east.

He focused on the rearview mirror. Traffic stacked up behind him. None of the cars stayed with him, but he couldn't be sure. He slammed on the brakes to avoid the car that slowed in front of him. Better concentrate on driving. He took the next exit. Did any of the cars following him look familiar? He didn't think so.

He drove into a gas station. While he swiped his card and filled the gas tank, he studied the highway and the exit ramp. Cars were veering off and maneuvering into the station. No one paid him any attention. He shook the nozzle and tightened the gas cap while glancing around. Still, everyone went about their business. If anyone had followed, they must have figured he was leaving and went back to Carlo. Or no one had been watching in the first place. To be sure, he removed the binoculars from his glove compartment and, staying as low as possible in the seat, searched again. Everything was normal. Now to implement his plan.

He kept to the back roads and parked a block behind Rossetti's—far enough away to go unseen but close enough to train his binoculars on the exit. He stayed in the car and watched.

And watched.

Nothing happened.

Was coming here a huge waste of time? He started to fold the binoculars, when the back door opened. He refocused quickly. Carlo exited! Tony waited while Carlo got into his Ferrari and left the lot. Once Carlo rounded the corner, Tony eased from the curb. By the time he reached the corner, he glimpsed Carlo's taillights as the car turned again. Trying to keep it in sight, he stayed back. Following someone was harder than it appeared on TV.

Soon Carlo chose a main road and other traffic surrounded him, so Tony relaxed. But he almost missed the turn when he couldn't change lanes in time. Where was Carlo going? Wouldn't it be his luck if he followed him around all day and nothing happened? His grandmother would be worried when he didn't arrive on time. Maybe he could call and tell her he had a flat. Who did he think he was anyway, Sherlock Holmes? He was certainly not a detective. Look what had been going on in his own house, and he didn't have a clue. What made him think he could catch someone like Carlo? And what would he do if he did?

He had about decided to stop the chase when Carlo swerved to the side of the road, stopped, and got out. What was he doing? Was he meeting someone? Maybe Tony could see who and then take off. Then he could call Mark from his grandmother's and give him a description. Feeling good, he stopped a half a block down.

Carlo had already gone into an ugly pink house.

As Tony approached, he saw that the blue front door was open. Paint peeled from it, and Tony feared the screen would squeak. Gingerly, he tugged it toward him. The walls were covered in a yellow film, and the place smelled like old cigarette smoke. He thought he heard something on his left so he followed, his tennis shoes making little creaks on the bubbled linoleum.

He was concentrating so hard on being silent, he didn't immediately realize he couldn't hear Carlo. In fact, he couldn't hear anything except his own breathing. He'd better go back to the car and wait. Maybe the person Carlo came to meet would go out with him, and Tony could get a picture with his phone.

As he turned to go, he glimpsed a figure from the corner of his eye moments before something slammed into him, knocking him sideways. His head hit the wall, and someone yanked his arm behind his back and twisted. A man's arm folded around his neck. The smell of Carlo's aftershave enveloped him.

"What are you doing, Tony?" The whisper next to his ear lifted the hair on Tony's neck.

He grunted. Sharp pain radiated through his shoulder.

"What? Cat got your tongue? Why aren't you with Granny? I warned your father about you. You're nothing but trouble."

"Let me go!" Tony jammed his other elbow back. Carlo jerked his arm again, and Tony sucked in his breath at the pain. He stood still.

"That's better. If you don't behave, I'll have to break it, and I don't want to." Tightening his grip around Tony's neck, Carlo released his arm but kept it pinned against his body. It offered immediate relief, but no room to move it to the front.

A second later, something hard poked Tony's ribs. He lowered his gaze. Sure enough, it was a gun.

"You've really messed up this time. I have half a

mind to shoot you right here and get it over with. But I might be able to use you later, so I'm giving you a chance." He moved his arm away from Tony's neck and placed a hand on his shoulder, giving him a push.

Tony stumbled along the narrow hallway and around the corner. Steps led to an open basement door. Carlo kept his hand on Tony's shoulder as he moved down the stairs, and at the bottom, Carlo gave him a shove.

Tony tried to bring his arm around, but it was stuck. He put the other hand out to stop his face from hitting the cement, but he twisted and landed on his sore arm. Pain shot through his shoulder. When he rolled over on his face, his arm loosened, and he managed to pull it around. He sat up and rubbed his shoulder, cradling his arm in his lap.

Carlo laughed. "Did I hurt your *wittle* arm?" He sneered. "Maybe it'll teach you to do what you're told."

He stepped back and slammed the door. The lock clicked.

37

Anger continued boiling inside Robin. She composed her features, forcing the anger to a simmer. Beth had cried while Mark lay there, silent, maybe dying, and Robin had believed her. Maybe Beth cried because she didn't want to do it. Maybe she was forced, and they could work out something together. She wanted to ask, but where to start?

"I know you won't believe me, but I never wanted to hurt Mark." Beth solved the dilemma.

Robin angled her body toward her. "Did someone threaten you? You don't have to do this. We can work something out. I'm sure the chief will want to help."

Beth laughed. "Threaten me? No."

"Then why did you give information to the drug dealers? Why did you tell them Mark was awake? That's why they tried to kill him, right? Because they found out through you he was awake?"

"Well, yes and no." Beth rounded a corner. "Renee Jackson was on duty, and she was infatuated with Jack. I needed to make the most of that. I told them he needed to go. But that clown, Oscar, botched it and got himself caught. How do you mess up a clean shot at ten feet? The moron. I should've done it myself, but taking care of the guard was risky enough. If he'd seen me, he would've recognized me, although that was part of the fun."

"You were there?" Robin decided to play along. "How did you deal with the guard? I got sketchy details from Mark, but I'm not sure he knows what happened."

"I'd been there a lot, watching. If anyone asked, I could say I was concerned about Mark. But no one saw me. I watched everyone, and Jack was popular with the nurses. He flirted with them all, but Renee gave him the most attention. She neglected her duties when he was around. So she became integral to my plan." She curved to the right.

Robin frowned. Her face wasn't covered. If she could see where Beth was going, did it mean Beth would kill her?

"Anyway," Beth continued. "That night I dressed up as a nurse and waited in an empty room until Jack went in to use the restroom. He did it a couple of nights I stayed over, so I assumed it was routine."

Robin squirmed. Someone spying on her when she was asleep gave her the creeps. Beth was right. Jack came in every night before she turned the light out, and she didn't notice him coming in again until morning. How often had Beth been down the hall watching?

"I ground up some of Aunt Janice's sleeping pills into a baggie, slipped them into some coffee, and set it next to his chair," Beth continued her story. "He thought Renee brought him a fresh cup, and he drank it. It didn't take long because I put in three times the dosage Aunt Janice uses. After all, Jack's a big guy. Oscar was supposed to go right in. But he waited too long, and Peter came in and, well, you know the rest."

Robin didn't know what to say, so she kept quiet.

Beth shrugged. "Everyone assumed the leak in the

department was someone who passed on information to the boss. I didn't have to tell the boss anything." She stared into Robin's eyes. "I am the boss."

Robin blinked and stifled a gasp. When she talked about ordering the hit on Mark, Robin got the impression Beth was passing on orders given to her. She tried to keep her voice even. "How did you go from being a trusted police administrative assistant to being a criminal? I don't understand."

"No one does. That's the beauty of it. My real father was killed committing a burglary when I was two years old, and my aunt and uncle raised me. They were nice people and all, but they never could get ahead. The story was that my father died in a car wreck and I took their last name. No one ever knew. I knew though. They never lied to me."

Beth turned toward the poorer side of town. "I could see people thought I wasn't too bright when I started working for the chief, so I used it to my advantage. I uncovered the names of my father's friends from some old papers I found and got in touch with them. I learned a few things along the way, and pretty soon, I was running the show." She stopped for a breath. The words spilled out as if she'd been waiting to tell someone. As though she needed someone to know how smart she was. It must have been difficult hiding it for so long.

"Nobody ever suspected the lowly secretary. And being blonde didn't hurt. I could pretend I didn't quite get it, and they bought it—hook, line, and sinker. I'm not sure Mark bought the dumb routine though. Greg believed it, and David used to take advantage of it, flirting with me and thinking I wouldn't tell on him when he turned stuff in half done. I finished them up and never told the chief. David was supposed to take the fall. His unfinished reports allowed me to make changes he wouldn't have wanted. Before long, I could have gotten rid of him. And when the chief wanted to know what happened, I could've produced incriminating reports. Being the dumb blonde that I am, no one would've expected me to see what was right in front of my face."

"Why Mark then?"

"He was in the wrong place at the wrong time. I'm not sure how he knew to go to the warehouse, but I did what I had to do. I guess it doesn't matter now." Beth was no longer talking. She was obviously thinking aloud.

Robin tried to be quiet, hardly breathing, so Beth would forget she was there.

"Now I guess I'll need to implement plan B." She fell silent again.

Robin moved her wrists. The tape pulled. What was plan B? And how did it involve her?

Beth drew up at the curb in front of an abandoned house. She turned off the car and came around to let Robin out. "Now don't get any ideas. No one's around, and if they were, they wouldn't care. I could shoot you on the street, and no one would even notice. So go quietly, and everything will be OK."

Beth's face carried an expression unlike any Robin had seen there before—almost clean of emotion—and her eyes glinted like ice pellets stuck in her head. Greg had been right. Getting this close to a murderer wasn't a good idea.

Robin approached the door without another word. Beth started to move around her when the door burst open from the inside. A small man with a pockmarked face glowered at them. Where had she seen him before?

"I'll take care of her if you want to get things set up," he said.

Beth nodded and handed him the gun. He nudged Robin into a hallway with stairs at the end. She tottered down the steps, her tied hands impairing her balance. The guy reminded her of the little boys in school who used to trip her and her friends then laugh when they got hurt. She would bet he wasn't the gentle type. She reached the bottom safely, and he stepped around and unlocked the door. He motioned for her to open it, and she brought her taped hands up, fit the knob between them, and turned. As it opened, he shoved her from behind. Her hands broke her fall, but she still ground her elbow into the cement floor.

As she expected, he laughed as he slammed the door and locked it.

"Mrs. Clayton?"

Sunlight streamed in the high window, its glare obscuring the speaker.

"Tony? Is that you? What are you doing here?" She rolled over and sat up. "If you're here, you're in as much trouble as I am, and that's not a good thing. But I have to admit, I'm happy to see you."

Tony knelt beside her. "Here, let me get that tape off." He tried to pull it gently, but even so all the hair came with it. She rubbed her wrists and then her shoulder.

"How did you get here?" he asked.

She told him about Beth, and he told her about Carlo.

"Well, now we know the connection, not that it'll help at this point," she said. "I don't think they're staying around long. Beth knows they suspect her at the station."

"At least Mark will be safe now if they leave." Tony wrapped his arms around his knees. "I don't know why they kept trying to kill him. It's not like he remembered anything." His face mirrored her frustration.

"I think they're afraid he might, and they didn't want to take a chance."

"They caught the guy, right?" he said.

"Yes, but he's not talking about who hired him."

"I think Carlo hired him, and I think I saw him do it. It's one of the things that made me suspicious of Carlo in the first place. I saw him hand a man something and say 'half now and half after.' I didn't think about it at the time. Then a whole bunch of other things happened, and I ended up here."

"Does Carlo know you saw him?"

"No. I don't think I'd be alive right now if he did. He only knows about me following him this morning."

"How do you know Carlo? And how did you know to follow him?"

He lowered his head until it touched his knees, and she could barely hear him. "You see, my family is involved."

"Involved? How?"

He lifted his head. "I didn't want to see it, but it explains a few things. My dad always wanted a successful business. My mom is a great cook, but it takes money to make a place like Rossetti's really nice."

"So they started dealing?" She kept her voice soft, afraid to scare him out of talking.

"They were storing it at the restaurant. My parents

didn't have to do anything at first, but then they started asking for more and more from my dad. They involved my brother more as an insurance policy than anything else. I would've been next. I think the only way they could trust my dad was if he had too much to lose."

He flexed his arm and rubbed his shoulder. "They were trying to get me involved, but my mother had a fit, and they backed off. I think they thought she'd chuck it all and tell on them if they went too far." He smiled. "She would have, too." The smile slipped from his face. "But how far is too far? Dealing to kids? Murder? How far were my parents willing to go?"

"What will you do?" Robin asked.

"I don't know yet, but I can't live like them, Mrs. Clayton. I can't!" He covered his face with his hands. "I don't want to be afraid all the time. My dad and brother, and even my mother, are afraid and miserable. I didn't know it wasn't normal until I met Lucy's family. I want to be like them...and you and Mark."

"What do you mean?"

"You know, happy. And peaceful. And not afraid."

"You can have that, too."

"I know. The preacher says to know Christ is to know peace. But how do you know Christ? I mean isn't He like God or something?"

Robin smiled gently. "You just ask Him into your heart. Do you want to do that?"

"I don't know. I don't think he'll want the son of a drug dealer."

"Don't be too sure. He wanted Paul, and Paul was running around trying to kill Christians."

"He was? You mean the Paul in the Bible?"

"The very same. You see, he thought he was doing God's work until Jesus appeared to him and asked him why he was persecuting Him."

Tony was quiet for a while, obviously digesting what she'd said. "I don't know that I'm ready, but I'll think about everything you said."

38

"Robin? They've got Robin?" Mark slammed his fist down on the table. How could he have let them get to his wife? First, he'd failed Cindy and now Robin.

Peter flinched as if he'd slapped him. "I'm so sorry. If I'd known she was going to visit Janice, I would have stopped her. Libby said she had a doctor's appointment or something."

The pain on Peter's face calmed him.

"It's not your fault," Mark said. "It's my fault. That's exactly the kind of thing Robin does. I should have known. I should have protected her." Mark jumped up and threw on the coat Lenny had bought him. "Let's go."

Peter grabbed his keys. "Where?"

"Rossetti's."

"You think they know where she is?"

"I think they know more than they're telling, and I'm sick of being nice." Mark flew out the door and jumped into Peter's SUV.

Peter followed, barely stopping to shut the cabin door. He raced down the dirt road, skidding around the corners. "Better call it in," he said.

"That didn't go so well for me last time," Mark said. "But now that Beth's not there, I guess I'm safe. This time I'm calling dispatch."

He pulled the radio from Peter's dash and called

in their location and where they were headed.

The restaurant was busy when they slammed through the doors. "May I help you?" The hostess asked as they whizzed by.

Peter flipped his badge at her. "No, we'll find our own table."

Mark took the stairs two at a time, with Peter following so close he clipped his heels. He slammed into Carlo's office. The door banged against the wall and came back at him. No one there.

Dominic stood outside his office. "What's this about?"

Mark charged him, and he backed out of the hallway and into his office, a frightened look on his face.

"Where is she?" Mark yelled.

"Who?" Dominic hurried into his office and put his desk between them. "Who are you looking for?"

A growl formed in Marks throat as he moved around the desk. "My wife! Where is she? I know you have her."

Dominic backed against the credenza, desperation in every line of his face. "I don't know! Calm down, I don't know what you're talking about."

A surge of adrenaline rolled over Mark as he pulled his bad arm out of the sling and grabbed Dominic's collar with both hands. He backed him in the corner, nowhere to go. He wanted to hit him, to smash him in the face until he told what he knew.

Someone put a restraining hand on his arm. He jerked his arm away and reared back, ready to slam his fist into whoever was trying to stop him from getting to his wife.

"Hey man, I'm on your side." Peter took a step

back and held up his hands.

Mark lowered his fists and tried to get his breathing under control. He stepped away from Dominic, afraid he wouldn't be able to control himself if he didn't put some distance between them. "Sorry," he said to his friend.

Peter grinned. "We'll keep that in reserve. Meanwhile," his gaze bored into Dominic's, who looked ready to wet himself, "you have some explaining to do." Peter allowed Dominic to sit, probably to keep him from falling.

Mark breathed slowly, in through his nose, out through his mouth, forcing himself to calm down.

Peter sat in one of the chairs at Dominic's desk, and Mark perched on the edge of the other.

Dominic eyed them like a deer watching a cougar. "What do you want?"

"Do you know the whereabouts of Mrs. Clayton?" Peter spoke first.

"No, I don't even know her."

"What about Beth Harris?"

"Who?"

By the total confusion on Dominic's face, he either didn't know who Beth was, or he was a fantastic actor.

Mark imagined it was the former. It made sense that Beth wouldn't want people to know who she was. It was far too dangerous. And he'd bet Carlo was the brains behind Rosetti's business. At least the illegal part. Maria probably ran the restaurant. Dominic didn't look as if he could run anything.

Peter had been questioning Dominic, to no avail.

Mark weighed his options. He interrupted. "Where's Carlo Litzi?"

39

Tony thought about what Robin said. His stomach lurched. How could his family be so evil? And how could he have ignored it? He remembered watching people at church when they repeated the prayer the pastor prayed about forgiving their sins. They looked so happy. He felt so dirty. He never realized it before, but now he wanted the feeling to go away. He wanted to feel clean.

He jolted as steps thudded outside and the lock rattled. Before he could move, Carlo had a gun pointed at him. A man Tony didn't know walked toward him with a rope and some burlap.

Tony's every muscle tensed.

"Settle down," Carlo said. "Don't do anything you'll regret. We're taking a little trip, and then maybe you can give me a hand. You don't want me to have to hurt this nice lady, do you?"

Tony forced his shoulders down and opened his clenched fists.

"That's better. Now put your hands behind you so Evan, here, can tie them."

The big muscle-bound man with legs the size of tree trunks lumbered over. What was Evan's day job? Wrestling? Bouncing at some lowlife bar? Gritting his teeth, Tony complied.

Evan tied his hands while Carlo held the gun on

Robin. Then the big man used the other end of the rope to tie her hands in front of her. Three feet of rope hung loose between them.

"Now if you're careful, you won't hurt yourselves. You follow Evan, and I'll follow you. How does that sound?" Carlo's voice held a cheerful ring, as though he was giving candy to a child.

Evan went to the door and waited for them to catch up.

Tony had to walk first, and Robin followed. If he went too fast, the rope pulled painfully on his arms. If he went too slow, she stepped on his heels. By the time they mounted the stairs, they were in sync. At the top, they turned left, went through the kitchen, and out to the garage toward a van with blacked out back windows. Carlo ordered them into the middle row of seats.

Getting in while tied together proved tricky. He nearly fell as Robin climbed in and the rope tightened, pulling him backward. Once they were seated, Evan untied Tony's hands and retied them in front. He then buckled first his seatbelt, then Robin's, and shook out the burlap. It unfolded as two bags.

"No!" Robin screamed. "Don't put that thing over my face." She jerked her head around, and Evan slapped her.

"Hey, knock it off!" Tony tried to rise. The seatbelt stopped him, and then Evan punched him in the face. His head snapped back, and pain exploded from his cheek.

Robin cried out, "Tony, no! It's OK. I'll wear it. Don't hurt him. Please don't hurt him."

That and Carlo's laughter were the last things Tony heard before he blacked out.

40

Dominic's face developed a sheen. He rubbed a hand over his forehead. It was shaking.

Mark smiled. Good.

"I don't know where he is. Did you check his office?"

"Yeah, Sherlock, we did that," Peter answered.

Dominic reached for the phone on his desk. "Here, let me page him." He pushed a button and spoke into the handset. "Carlo, come to Dominic's office, Carlo Litzi to Dominic's office."

The words came to Mark in stereo, followed by a click after he hung up. Mark's arm twitched, and pain blossomed from his shoulder. He slipped it back into the sling.

"Arm hurting? Hope you didn't pull out the stitches." Dominic fumbled in his drawer. "I think I have some aspirin in here, somewhere." Suddenly, he was so eager to please. This might go better than he thought.

"It's nothing," Mark said. No time to worry about stitches now.

They waited in silence for a few minutes.

Mark, unable to sit still any longer, leapt to his feet and started pacing. He wasn't here, the dirt bag wasn't here, because he was somewhere holding Robin. He turned to Dominic, wanting to choke the answers out of him. "Where would he go?" he asked. "If he kidnapped someone, where would he take her?"

Dominic's face paled. "Kidnapping? I don't know anything about any kidnapping."

Maria Rossetti burst through the door, followed by their son, Jimmy. She skidded to a stop when she saw Mark and Peter.

"Tony's missing." Her voice was high and shaky.

Dominic glanced up at her, ready to dismiss her. "Give him time. He probably stopped somewhere to eat." He nodded to Peter. "Gentlemen, my wife, Maria. Maria, this is the police." His voice delivered a warning, but she didn't seem to care.

"Good. I'd like to report a missing person."

"Maria, I don't think that's necessary."

She turned on him and brandished her nails, as if to launch an attack. "I don't care what you think! I've had enough. If Carlo hurts a hair on my boy's head, I swear, I'll kill him myself!"

Jimmy winced but remained silent.

Mark wondered what he knew.

"Maria!" Dominic tried again to shut her up.

"Mrs. Rossetti," Peter said. "Tell us what happened."

She glanced over at her husband and back to Peter. "He was supposed to go straight to his grandmother's. He should have been there hours ago. Katherine said he never made it."

"When did she call?" Peter's voice was too calm.

Mark wanted to jerk the information out of her.

"The first time was a couple hours ago, and I told her to wait awhile in case he ran into some bad traffic or something. She called a few minutes ago and said he's still not there."

"What do you think happened?" Peter asked. "Did you try his cell phone?"

"Yes, but all I get is voice mail. I'm worried about him, Dominic. I don't know what to think."

Jimmy wiped his hands on his jeans. He knew something.

Maria dialed her cell. "Tony, this is your mother. It isn't funny now. Call me." Her voice trembled. "Please, honey, you're scaring me." The fear in the woman's voice was palpable.

Mark could feel it emanating out of her.

"Do you think Carlo would hurt him?" Dominic asked.

"If he thinks Tony's a threat..." Mom's voice drifted off. "Look what happened to that Joey kid last year. He was just a baby."

"Come on now," Dominic said. "We don't know what happened to that kid. Maybe he wasn't getting better like they thought."

"Right, Einstein. He was doing fine. Then we heard the chief was going to talk to him, and the next thing you know his funeral's in the paper."

This was getting interesting. But they didn't have time to investigate that right now, they needed to find Carlo.

"Where would Carlo take him?" Mark asked, careful do dial back on the anxiety he felt.

The backup he'd called for could be heard in the hallway.

Dominic didn't want to answer.

"There's a meeting place he uses, an old school in the process of remodel. Or he uses the warehouse in Denver," Jimmy spilled the truth.

Denver seemed the obvious place, and Mark could

tell Peter thought so, too. He bounded out of his chair. "What's the address?"

Dominic gave them a blank stare. Mark couldn't tell if he was being obstinate or if he just couldn't remember. He opened the credenza behind him and fumbled through some papers.

"I can take you there," Jimmy said. "I need to know my little brother's OK."

Mark, Peter and Jimmy ran from the room, passing the other officers. "Hold them for questioning," Peter said. "We'll call from the road and explain."

41

Tony woke in the van, his head aching. He couldn't see. What was this thing over his face? Then it all came back. He hoped Robin was OK. She was quiet next to him, probably praying. It sounded like a good idea. He wished his grandmother was here. She prayed great prayers, as if she knew God personally or something. Since she wasn't here, he wished he could pray. But he knew God wouldn't want to talk to him. Then he remembered what Robin said about Paul. If he had wanted to talk to Paul, maybe he would give Tony a chance. After all, Tony hadn't killed any Christians.

He considered his grandmother. He wanted what she had. He wanted to be able to talk to God like a real person. He needed someone who would love him despite his family. Someone who wouldn't let him down. Someone who wouldn't do the wrong thing for money.

He knew where he could go to get that. He would talk to his grandmother as soon as he got out of here. *But what if I don't get out of this? What about now? I know what to do. I've seen it at church, and Grandmother told me how. Why not do it now?*

He'd always planned to become a Christian someday. All those summers with his grandmother convinced him long ago that he wanted to grow up like her. Then his friends at church made it feel even more possible. He closed his eyes and prayed the words he hoped would change his life.

Jesus, I know I'm a sinner. And I know You don't need someone like me. But I need You. I might not get this right, but please come into my heart and make me Your child.

He opened his eyes and then quickly shut them. *Thank You. In Jesus' name, amen.* They always said that at church. It seemed too simple. Was that all there is to it? Peace seeped into his heart.

Yes, that's all there is to it.

42

Robin tried to remain calm. The van had made a few turns, then accelerated, as if on the highway. She lost track of the length of time they stayed on the highway, but wherever they were going must be pretty far away from Pinon Creek.

Tony had been silent most of the trip, moaning a little in the last half hour or so. She hoped he was all right. That Neanderthal had hit him pretty hard.

Finally, the van turned off and made several more turns before coming to a stop and shutting down. The sound of metal and gears grinding together led her to believe they had entered a garage of some sort.

The van door slid open and the bag over her head was removed. Fresh air caressed her face. Well not outside fresh air, but better than what she'd been breathing through the burlap. A couple times she almost panicked, a smothered feeling almost overcoming her. The only way she was able to stand it was to close her eyes and practice breathing, in and out, in and out.

The Neanderthal stood in front of them holding a gun. He pulled the bag off Tony's head, and she was relieved to see he was awake. His cheek was red and swollen, and his nose had bled down his face. Neanderthal unlatched her seatbelt and Tony's. "Get out," he growled. He waved the gun toward Tony.

"You, too. And don't try nothing, or you'll get more of that." He pointed the gun at Tony's cheek as if to touch it, but Tony ripped his head back. The Neanderthal laughed.

Robin struggled out of her seat, trying not to jerk too hard on the rope. She and Tony stumbled and nearly fell out of the van and onto the concrete floor of a large warehouse. Double doors had closed them in, and there was another set next to those with room to park a couple large trucks. Flickering fluorescents barely lit the huge area, but after being in almost total darkness, she could see pretty well. Metal shelving stacked with boxes towered on her right. Ahead of her sat Beth's yellow sports car. So, she was here.

Carlo slammed the driver's side door and nodded to Neanderthal. "Take care of these two, would you?"

Her heart slammed in her chest. What did that mean?

"What do you want me to do with them?"

"Put them in the cafeteria for now. Tie them to something."

Neanderthal tied them the same way they were before and motioned for them towards another area.

Tony started walking. He moved too fast and yanked her hands. She moved too slow and heard his hiss of pain as his arms jerked back. After a few steps, they got in rhythm, and it was easier.

An office with a window overlooking the warehouse occupied the center of the floor. A hallway ran next to it, which was where the body builder directed them to go. As they made their steady way in that direction, the other set of double doors opened.

Robin turned to look without slowing her progress.

An unmarked truck the size and shape of a medium U-Haul pulled in. The driver cut the engine, and the double doors thundered back down.

Robin took a last look around the warehouse before she reached the hallway. More rows of the same shelving lined this side of the warehouse, and a set of five overhead doors loomed on the other side of the warehouse. Loading docks? She wondered what they distributed here besides drugs.

At the end of the hallway, a door opened to a cafeteria, lined with long steel tables molded to include the benches as one piece. Massive bolts held each table to the concrete floor. Neanderthal forced her to sit at a table and bound her feet to the steel legs. He did the same with Tony on the other side of the table, facing her. He tested the ropes and laughed. "Don't you go nowhere, now, ya hear?" He left them alone, slamming the door behind him.

Robin could move her hands up and down, but the rope binding them to her feet kept her from resting them all the way on the table. With her ankles bound to the bench support, she couldn't move them. She wriggled her hands, working at the rope. The thick hemp wouldn't budge.

From Tony's movements, it appeared he was doing the same thing. "We've got to get out of here," he said. "I don't know what Carlo will do to my family now."

Robin didn't say what she was thinking. Why would he let either of them live? Especially her, since she knew who they were. It was a matter of time. Were the police looking for her? She had no idea of the time. Did they even know she was missing yet? She cleared her throat. "Won't someone be missing you soon?"

"My grandmother will miss me and call. I was supposed to be driving to her house." His shoulders jerked. Yep, he was trying to get loose. "I don't know what they'll do about it. No one will go against Carlo even if they figured out he grabbed me."

A scratching grated at the door. Robin dropped her hands in her lap.

Carlo came in. "Tony," he moved to his side of the table, "I need your help."

Tony shuddered. "You're kidding, right?"

Carlo's face hardened. "No, I'm not kidding." Then his lips pulled back in a smile that sent chills along Robin's spine. "But if you don't feel like doing it, you don't have to." He pulled a long, curved knife out of a sheath on his belt and studied the tip. "Did you know I can get your brother put away for murder? All it takes is one little call and the gun planted in the right place, and little Jimmy goes away for good. Is that what you want?"

"No." Tony scowled at the floor. "What do you want me to do?"

"That's more like it. I knew you'd see it my way." Carlo reached down and cut the rope around Tony's feet. "If you try anything funny, I'll kill you and send your brother to jail. Then your parents will lose two children."

Tony nodded. "What about Mrs. Clayton? If I help you, will you let her go?"

Robin held her breath. What was he doing? He would get himself killed!

Carlo glanced at her as if she were a cockroach at his dinner party. "Mrs. Clayton is not your concern. Don't you worry. I'm sure we can find a use for her."

Tony pressed his lips tight, as if he wasn't too sure,

but he must have thought she was safe for the moment because he let himself be led away.

Robin remembered what he had tried to do for her in the van—and had gotten punched for his efforts. *God, please don't let that boy get killed protecting me.* What were Carlo's exact words? Did he mean they had something for her to do, or was he humoring Tony into doing what he wanted? She lowered her face and rubbed it on her arm, to scratch the itch on her nose. What could she possibly do?

Mark! The only use for her was Mark. They would use her as a hostage to get him out of hiding. Thank goodness, they didn't know about the baby. They would have even more leverage then. But what was she thinking? Heat rose in her face, a shameful heat. It wouldn't matter whether Mark knew about the baby or not, he'd come out of hiding for her. He would give his life for hers. She knew how much he loved her. How could she have doubted him? Beth knew what kind of man he was, yet Robin, his own wife, had doubted him. She clawed at the knots again. She couldn't let that happen.

The rope gave a little. With new vigor she tugged, pulled and clawed harder, her fingers bending backward and her nails snagging and tearing on the rough hemp. Attuned to every sound—her breath, her own heartbeat, the scratching rope—she worked, expecting someone to burst through the door any second. Her fingers had rubbed raw, their efforts seemingly futile...until the knots eased loose. She pulled them off and started on the ropes at her feet.

43

Tony moved his arms and rubbed his wrists. Carlo grabbed his elbow, jerked him forward, and pushed him through the door, still holding his arm in a vise grip.

"No funny business now, or I'll have to mess up that pretty-boy face of yours." His eyes were black and deep.

Did Carlo want him to try something so he could prove how macho he was? He trudged along with him. Then Carlo lifted a dolly from the truck next to the van they arrived in. His arms flexed and bulged.

Man, he really was strong. Fighting him wouldn't be such a good idea. Time to dismiss any vague thoughts of overpowering him and taking the knife.

"I want you to load this truck with those boxes." Carlo pointed to the right.

"What's in them?"

"Jars of sauce. What else?" He gave the shark grin. "Don't worry. This shipment isn't going to Pinon Creek. This one's staying in Denver."

So they were in Denver. Not that it helped, but knowing felt better. "You mean you send it other places?"

"Yeah, I guess you could say I'm in the big league now." He swaggered around the truck. "Multiple locations to serve you."

The creep was proud of it, as though he had a chain of stores or something. He jerked his head toward the boxes and leaned against the truck.

While Tony stacked boxes on the dolly, Carlo pretended to clean his nails with the knife. He watched Tony manhandle the heavy dolly up the ramp and move it into position in the rear of the truck. After Tony stacked a second load, hauled it into the truck, and came out, Carlo was gone.

Tony filled his lungs. Without those bottomless black eyes staring at him, maybe he could think of a way out. He couldn't be a part of this, and he couldn't let them hurt Robin. But what about Jimmy? How could he help Robin and still keep Jimmy out of jail? What an impossible situation.

As he shoved the next load into the truck, a woman crept from the hallway and disappeared into a row of boxes. Startled, he nearly tipped the dolly.

Robin got loose! Good, maybe she could go get help. Tony frowned. If they found her, they'd hurt her. Or worse. They certainly didn't have any problem with murder. What could he do?

He peered at the darkness between the boxes on the shelves. Was that her? He didn't think so. She'd disappeared. Maybe she got out. No, if the door opened, he'd have seen the light. And so would Carlo. An idea occurred to him. He'd create a diversion.

Tony unloaded the boxes he had and rolled the dolly down the ramp. This time he loaded four boxes instead of three and shoved hard to get the dolly to move. It did a little. Then the weight of the boxes helped him get a run at the ramp. He went at it at a slight angle, and he was almost to the top when the dolly tipped sideways and the boxes flew off.

44

Robin slid between the boxes and sighed with relief. She felt safer out of the open. Now how could she get out? She walked the length of the shelves and peered around the end. Tony stacked boxes on a dolly and loaded them on a truck. She looked around her. What could she use to defend herself? Too bad there wasn't a loaded gun just lying on a shelf somewhere.

She edged back the way she'd come, around the end and into the next one. Her hopes fell as she padded along, finding nothing useful. A metal pipe about three feet long that must have been part of the shelving caught her eye. It rested on a shelf as if placed there and forgotten. She eased it up and weighed it in her hand. It wouldn't stop a bullet, but it was better than nothing. She tightened her grip on it, the metal cutouts pinching against her palms. At least she wasn't totally helpless.

A loud crash clattered from the truck. Seconds later four men burst out of a doorway and ran toward the sound. Carlo was with them. Good. If that was all the men, then she only had to worry about Beth. If that was all. Carlo started shouting at Tony, and she inched around the shelving. So how would she get Tony and get out? She saw a side door and almost took it. But there was no way she could leave Tony. There had to be a better way.

Beth ran from the hallway. "Where's Robin?" she screamed. "She's gone!"

Robin peered through the boxes.

Carlo glanced up from watching Tony sweep each tiny bit of white powder into a container.

"Calm down. I put her in the old lunchroom."

"No! She's not there. I looked." Beth's voice was so high and squeaky Robin hardly understood her.

Carlo ambled over, said something, and stroked her arms. Robin couldn't hear, but whatever he said calmed her. They gazed around the warehouse.

Robin ducked below the boxes.

"Hey, Lou!" Carlo yelled as he walked toward someone who had entered the office behind the glass. Lou stood and met Carlo at the door. He then went back inside, grabbed something from a drawer, and handed it to Carlo. Robin couldn't see it until Carlo gave it to Beth—a gun.

Lou yelled, "Wait. That's not—"

Carlo scowled. "She knows it's not a toy. Do you think she's never used one before?"

Lou stood there mouth still open, closed it, shook his head, and then backed into the office. In no time, he returned with a gun of his own sticking out of his waistband. The three split up and moved toward different parts of the warehouse.

Robin's heart leapt in her chest. What could she do? Shelves of boxes towered around her. Stairs led to the second floor, but in all the movies where the heroine went up instead of down, she trapped herself. Better stay here. She carefully laid the pipe she had been carrying on a shelf and climbed up beside it, huddling between two large boxes. The boxes were stacked two deep along each row. She sat frozen with her feet up, trying to blend.

She could barely see above the boxes along the row, and ducked as the man they called Lou passed her row, glanced down it, and kept going. She released her breath. She had to do something. She couldn't stay here forever. She'd be caught. Could she sneak into the back of the truck, get Tony, and get out? Her courage almost failed her. It was suicide. She thought of her unborn baby. She'd rather they died trying than to have him or her know its mother was a coward. She rubbed her stomach. *Please God, now's the time for a miracle.*

She gingerly stepped down and retrieved the pipe, tiptoeing toward the truck, trying to keep out of sight. She was quiet, but so were the searchers.

The only sound was Tony loading more boxes.

45

Tony paused from sweeping white powder into a clean dustpan and then into the container Carlo brought. He hoped they found a way to remove all the tiny shards of glass, since Carlo apparently planned to sell every last granule. He hadn't known what to do after hearing Beth scream, so he kept sweeping. He couldn't drag it out any longer though. He'd obviously scraped as much as humanly possible off the cement. He propped the broom against a shelf and went back to the dolly.

No one stopped him, so he loaded a box on the dolly, then another and started up the ramp. The search continued around him. He hoped Robin made it outside and away from the building. He froze as the side door opened. Was she getting out? Should he make a run for it or maybe try to create another distraction? No, if he did, it would only draw attention to something they might not have noticed.

Lou headed to the door.

Someone was coming in, not going out.

"Jimmy!" Lou said. "What're you doing here? How ya doin', man?"

Jimmy shook Lou's hand. "I'm good. I thought I'd stop by and see if you needed help."

"There's probably something you can do. Let me check with Carlo."

While Lou moved off to find him, Jimmy hurried to Tony. "Get in the truck. The cops are outside, but I need to get the overhead doors open."

"There's a woman here who needs help," Tony hissed.

"The cop's wife?"

"Yeah. How did you know?"

"That's who's outside. They didn't want to storm the place for fear of hurting either of you. I'm going to hit the doors. Yell for her as soon as I do." Jimmy walked over to the door opener and hit the button.

Tony yelled, "Robin! Get in the truck!"

Robin scrambled out of the row closest to the truck and raced toward him.

The woman they called Beth jumped out from a row of boxes and pointed her gun.

Robin dropped the pipe she'd been carrying and raised both hands.

He heard a click. Nothing.

Beth looked at her gun and tried again. Click.

A shot rang out from somewhere behind Beth and imbedded itself in a box next to Robin's head.

Robin grabbed the pipe and swung it at Beth. It connected, and Beth flew backward, hitting a shelf and knocking it over.

Tony sprinted to the cab of the truck and yanked open the passenger door. Another bullet hit the door as he jumped in.

Robin scurried up the ramp and the sliding door clattered as she struggled to tug it down. He was crouching on the floor, when he saw the keys dangling from the ignition. He reached over and started the truck.

The driver's side door flew open, and Jimmy

jumped inside, staying low.

"Thanks, buddy." Jimmy threw the truck into reverse. The ramp screeched as Jimmy floored the gas and the truck leapt backward.

Tony peered over the dash. They cleared the doors and most of the parking lot by the time Jimmy slammed on the brakes. Tony did a face plant on the dash.

Police converged from each side of the garage door, yelling and brandishing guns.

When Tony raised his head farther, he saw Mark running toward him, his arm still in a sling. "She's in the back!" Tony yelled.

Mark changed direction as Tony dropped to the pavement. Blood dripped from his nose. He swiped it with the back of his hand as he raced around the truck, meeting Mark at the back. Each grabbed a side of the sliding door and hauled it up.

"Robin, are you in here?" Mark craned his neck and peered in. He pressed his good arm against the edge of the truck and prepared to vault inside.

She crawled out from among the boxes and stepped around the mangled ramp, still precariously attached. He held up his good arm, grasped her hand, and steadied her as she jumped down. She threw her arms around him and burst into tears.

Tony turned to give them some privacy. Jimmy! With a gasp, Tony dashed to the driver's side.

A Denver policeman eased Jimmy carefully out of the truck. Blood soaked the left side of his pants.

"Jimmy, what happened? Did you get shot?"

"I think I got hit by a ricochet. It's OK though. It just skimmed me. What about you? You're bleeding."

Tony took another swipe at his nose. It came away

red.

A waiting ambulance skidded to a stop beside them.

"It's nothing. How'd you know where I was?" Tony asked.

"When you hadn't shown up at Grandma's yet, I took a chance you'd be here away from the heat in Pinon Creek."

The EMTs pulled a gurney from the ambulance and half-lifted Jimmy onto it. "You'd better get in here with us, son," one of them said. "It's safer in here." He handed Tony a clean gauze patch and reached out to help him up.

Tony put the gauze up to his nose, climbed into the ambulance, and moved to a corner out of the way of bullets but still next to Jimmy. "You risked your life for me?"

Jimmy grimaced while they cut his jeans away from the gash in his leg, cleaned, and bandaged it. "It's my fault you got into this mess. If I hadn't been stupid enough to trust Carlo and let him bully me, you wouldn't be here."

Carlo and his friends were in handcuffs, and the police were readying them for the ride to jail.

Not needing to go to the hospital, Jimmy sat on the ambulance bumper.

Tony lowered himself beside him, his nose sore but no longer bleeding. "It's not entirely your fault. If Dad hadn't decided dealing drugs was an acceptable way to make a living, none of us would be here."

Jimmy leaned his head back. "Yeah, I guess so. I'm tired of being scared. I don't care what they do to me. It's better than worrying about Carlo. I'm glad it's over."

46

Peter helped a handcuffed Beth climb into the back of an ambulance. "How's that jaw?" he asked.

"It's on fire. Robin probably broke it."

"Awww. Too bad."

She glared at him.

"I heard what happened in there. Sounds to me as if your boyfriend wants you dead."

She glowered at Carlo being loaded into a police car.

"Why else would he have given you an unloaded gun? Obviously Lou tried to tell him, but I heard Carlo cut him off."

He unlocked the handcuffs and relocked them, confining her to a gurney. "I've heard of hard breakups, but this was a little extreme, don't you think? He must have been ashamed of you—I've never seen you guys together."

"Keeping our relationship a secret was my decision."

Peter tried to look sympathetic. He was pretty sure he was failing.

"The first time his people saw me, they thought I was one of his women. It amused me."

"Didn't his having other women bother you?"

She tried to smile, but pain flitted across her face. "After all, I had other men. Wealthy men who took me to the restaurant where Carlo worked and then to the opera. I loved flaunting my boyfriends, making him jealous."

Peter waited for a uniformed Denver police officer to take his place then jumped down from the ambulance. Beth had a good thing going for a while, but it was destined to fail. She waited too long to leave. She must have felt she had the upper hand over Carlo. It was obvious they didn't love each other. The thought made him shiver. Wonder what Carlo would say to the police? Likely, anything he could to cut a deal. But then so would Beth. He shook his head. They deserved each other. He headed over to check on Mark and Robin. Now there was a relationship worth having.

47

Robin shifted.

Mark leaned back on the couch next to her, holding her hand. The TV droned on, but she wasn't watching. "I could have lost you." His voice was hoarse.

She must have cried the entire two days since he'd helped her out of the truck. What was it with these hormones anyway? She didn't think she had more tears in her, but her eyes fooled her again. She gave his hand another squeeze. "I can't imagine my life without you. The whole thing feels like a bad dream." She scanned the room. All Mark's things she hadn't liked as a decorator, now she wouldn't change for anything. They made the room a home.

"I still can't believe it was Beth."

"I can't believe you hit her with a pipe." He laughed. "All that batting practice must have done some good, eh?"

"It's funny, I know. I did it without thinking." She replayed a picture of Beth pointing the gun at her. "Why didn't her gun work?"

"Apparently the gun her boyfriend gave her wasn't loaded. Nobody knows why. He says it was because she was unstable, and he didn't want her to kill anyone else. He says she killed Cindy, and Beth says he killed her. They're all turning on each other now."

Copying his position, she leaned her head back against the couch. "No wonder she stuck her healthy, vibrant aunt into a nursing home. She didn't want her close enough to tell anyone about the money. What will happen to her now?"

"Janice? I don't know, but I think she'll want out of the home. She didn't belong there." He brought their clasped hands up and kissed the back of hers then lowered them to his lap.

"How did she take everything?"

"You know, she was pretty upset but not as surprised as I would have expected. I wonder if she knew there was something wrong with Beth while she was raising her."

Robin stared at the screen in front of her, the images passing before her eyes but not contacting her brain. "You know, I feel sorry for her. I believe Beth really did love her. What will she do now?"

"Sunny View is keeping her until she finishes physical therapy. Then she can do whatever she wants. I think she has enough original money—money unconnected to the drugs—that she can live comfortably. Not extravagantly like Beth was, but if she's careful, she'll be OK." He shifted his weight but didn't let go of Robin's hand.

"With everything going on, I haven't had a chance to ask. Do you remember any of what happened the day you got shot?"

"Yeah, I remember it all now. I was starting to recall bits and pieces of being in the warehouse and seeing briefcases on the table, and eventually it would have all come back. Beth couldn't take that chance, so she tried to have me killed. That jogged my memory, seeing the guy with the gun. Carlo was the one who shot me. Then things kept coming back to me until I remembered calling the chief and getting Beth."

"What happened before that, and why didn't you tell Peter or me?"

"I didn't mean to leave you guys out. Cindy called my cell phone as I was leaving the house. I was going in early to do some paperwork before the meeting, and I wanted to talk to the chief. Cindy sounded frantic and said she had followed them all night and they were in a warehouse. She figured out what they were doing and called me in a panic. She begged me to come alone. I knew I couldn't, but I wasn't sure who to trust. Peter, of course, but he wasn't on duty at that hour."

Mark let go of her hand to fold his arm around her. "I didn't believe it at first," he said. "We've had so many false alarms. But I didn't want to call it in, for fear of alerting the mole if it was real, and of bringing out the whole crew for nothing if it wasn't. Anyway, I called the chief's direct line. Instead, Beth answered and promised to get him right away and to get a hold of anyone he wanted to send without using dispatch. How ridiculous. If I'd called it in to dispatch, she wouldn't have found out about it in time to stop it. Instead, she alerted Carlo, and he was expecting me. Then she showed up looking for Cindy. She found and killed her." He lowered his head. "It's my fault Cindy's dead. If I had followed procedure, she'd be alive."

"That's not true, and you know it. You had no idea who the leak was. If you followed procedure, Cindy would still be dead because she was in way over her head. What was she doing following them? Did she tell you how she knew who to follow?"

"No. I'm not positive, but I think Dominic told her.

Then she started following Carlo. Oh, by the way, Tony identified the man who tried to shoot me in the hospital as the same man he saw Carlo pay. That ties Carlo in pretty securely. When he heard that, he started telling us Beth killed Cindy. I think he's trying everything he knows to get a lesser sentence. Neither he nor Beth are talking about their suppliers though. They must have them scared."

He relaxed his hold, keeping his arm draped over her shoulder, and rested his head back against the couch. "It won't matter. While you and Tony were in the warehouse, Dominic sang his guts out. He was so afraid Carlo would kill his sons, he didn't care what he was confessing to. As long as someone stopped Carlo, he didn't care."

"What about Maria and Jimmy? Are they being charged?"

"Maria will be, yes. She agreed to the operation in the beginning and went along with it the whole time. I think Jimmy will get some leniency. The DA is open to a lesser sentence for him since he risked his life to save you and his brother." His fingers caressed her arm. "I, for one, am very grateful to him."

"And Rossetti's? What will happen to the restaurant?"

"The IRS are sniffing around, so it'll probably be confiscated. I can't imagine Dominic reporting his drug money on his taxes." He turned his head to gaze at Robin, and his eyes were sad. "The whole family is cooperating, so we're going pretty far up the chain. It's nice to know something good came of this. Cindy would be happy if she knew."

"She does know, Mark. She's looking down now happy you finished what she began."

"She must've been pretty good when she followed them, because I don't think they knew she was there before I told Beth."

"Stop beating yourself up. You had no time to think, and you put your life at risk to save her. It isn't your fault you lived and she died." As she said it, she realized she'd found the source of Mark's guilt. He was supposed to protect Cindy, yet she'd died and he didn't. He'd eventually work his way through it but would always feel he failed.

She snuggled close. "So, what are we naming our child? Mark if it's a boy, I think. I love the name Mark."

He pulled her tighter. "You know, I think I'd like to name him Tony, if you don't mind, and Cindy if it's a girl."

Robin didn't even have to think about it. She smiled. "I think that's a great idea. Tony or Cindy it is."

A Devotional Moment

And if we are careful to obey all this law
before the Lord our God, as he has
commanded us, that will be our
righteousness. ~ Deuteronomy 6:25

A person can be caught up in unrighteousness without being the instigator of evil. Events occur that make us appear to be guilty when the opposite is true. We can be judged just by the company we keep. There are instances where keeping company with those who are unrighteous is necessary— the police undercover, ministers in the prison system, missionary outreaches to those who have fallen victim to prostitution or drug addiction. But even when we are called into these specialized instances, we must be careful to guard our hearts and minds—and in some instances, our physical self, as well. The Word cautions Christians about unsavory people. We are to be discerning about surrounding ourselves with people of good character. By doing so, we balance our own behavior so that those who seek God will want to be part of a wholesome community.

In **High Deceit**, the protagonist must battle for another person's character, and in so doing, must work against time to find resolutions. But others are actively against her efforts to righteously discern the truth. She must seek answers in places where angels fear to tread and pray that her life will not be taken or changed forever.

Does it seem difficult to see the fine line between embracing the broken and separating yourself from the lost? Know that the difference can be seen in the other person's desire to change. Christ reached out to all with mercy, but also said to all, "Go, and sin no more." When you reach out, guard yourself. Everyday friends should be righteous; it is necessary to have a righteous example and support system. But when you need to reach the unrighteous, reach out with mercy and correction. If their answer, by word or by deed, says that they do not want to change, then you must accept their choice and leave them before they pull you down with them.

LORD, TEACH ME TO SURROUND MYSELF WITH PEOPLE OF GOOD CHARACTER WHO ALSO WANT TO GROW IN SPIRIT AND THE WORD. GRANT ME THE KNOWLEDGE I NEED TO BE A HELP TO THE UNRIGHTEOUS AND TO KNOW IF IT'S TIME TO LEAVE. IN JESUS' NAME I PRAY, AMEN.

You Can Help!

At Pelican Book Group it is our mission to entertain readers with fiction that uplifts the Gospel. It is our privilege to spend time with you awhile as you read our stories.

We believe you can help us to bring Christ into the lives of people across the globe. And you don't have to open your wallet or even leave your house!

Here are 3 simple things you can do to help us bring illuminating fiction™ to people everywhere.

1) If you enjoyed this book, write a positive review. Post it at online retailers and websites where readers gather. And share your review with us at reviews@pelicanbookgroup.com (this does give us permission to reprint your review in whole or in part.)

2) If you enjoyed this book, recommend it to a friend in person, at a book club or on social media.

3) If you have suggestions on how we can improve or expand our selection, let us know. We value your opinion. Use the contact form on our web site or e-mail us at customer@pelicanbookgroup.com

God Can Help!

Are you in need? The Almighty can do great things for you. Holy is His Name! He has mercy in every generation. He can lift up the lowly and accomplish all things. Reach out today.

Do not fear: I am with you; do not be anxious: I am your God. I will strengthen you, I will help you, I will uphold you with my victorious right hand.

~Isaiah 41:10 (NAB)

We pray daily, and we especially pray for everyone connected to Pelican Book Group—that includes you! If you have a specific need, we welcome the opportunity to pray for you. Share your needs or praise reports at http://pelink.us/pray4us

Free Book Offer

We're looking for booklovers like you to partner with us! Join our team of influencers today and receive at least one free eBook per month. Maybe more!

For more information
Visit http://pelicanbookgroup.com/booklovers